EDUARDO ESPINOZA

is a medical doctor with a Master's in Public Health, Professor of Health Systems and Health Policy in the Master's in Public Health programme at the University of El Salvador and a health sector reform researcher. He was active in the revolutionary forces from 1975 to 1992 during the civil war in El Salvador, in charge of medical services in battle zones and of training health activists for the rebels and the civilian population in these areas, which had been abandoned by government medical services. He was detained and tortured twice: in 1978 (two months) and in 1985 (eight months). With the signing of the Peace Accords in 1992, he returned to the University of El Salvador to do research and teach public health. From 1995 to 1999, he was Dean of the Medical School at the University of El Salvador. He is a faculty member of the International People's Health University, a project of the People's Health Movement. In 2009, the government of the Farabundo Martí National Liberation Front (FMLN) party drafted him to join the cabinet as Deputy Minister for Health Policy, where he continues, now with the second FMLN administration, elected in 2014.

The Liberation Struggle in El Salvador

Eduardo Espinoza

The Liberation Struggle in El Salvador

A MEMOIR

LeftWord

Offset edition first published in November 2018
Digital print edition, January 2020

LeftWord Books
2254/2A Shadi Khampur
New Ranjit Nagar
New Delhi 110008
INDIA

LeftWord Books is the publishing division of
Naya Rasta Publishers Pvt. Ltd.

leftword.com

Translated by Susan C. Greenblatt

Footnotes by the translator have been marked as such (—*Tr.*). The rest of the notes were made by the author.

ISBN 978-93-80118-77-2

To
Nelly Cacao (Mextli)
Carlos Linares (Pedro)
Isis Dagmar Pocasangre (Sonia)
Ignacio Martín Baró (Chungo)
Ethel Pocasangre (Crucita)
Wilfredo Landaverde Monterrosa (Guille)
Ana Vilma Miranda (Silvia)
Iván Hernández (Hugo) (Tato)
Estela Benítez Hernández (Lupita)
Luis Ángel Ramírez Portillo (Lito)
Ana Margarita Peña Mendoza (Esther)
Laura Menéndez (Lorena)
Carlos Vargas
Blas
Alejandra Betancourt (Julia)
Andrés Dubón
Madeleine Lagadec

. . . and Elmer!

To my family, especially to my mother and my siblings, who endured humiliation, heartache, persecution and exile due to my dedication to the revolutionary cause (and continued to love me just the same).

To Jaime, my son, who accompanied me in my guerrilla wanderings at a very young age and who was the driving force of my efforts to help build a better world for those who will inherit it.

To the University of El Salvador, which taught me, giving me the tools and the capacity to produce knowledge to fight injustice, corruption, mediocrity and opportunism and to contribute to steering social action.

To Eduardo Galeano, whose *Open Veins of Latin America* was the ideological trigger that led me to join the revolutionary struggle.

To the ex-combatants, war wounded, lay health workers – *promotoras, brigadistas, sanitarios* – collaborators, international solidarity organizations, internationalists, the tortured, dead and disappeared, the orphans, the poor, the marginalized, those excluded from the global banquet,
and the new generations . . .

. . . trusting that they will forgive us for not having been able to finish the job

(yet).

CONTENTS

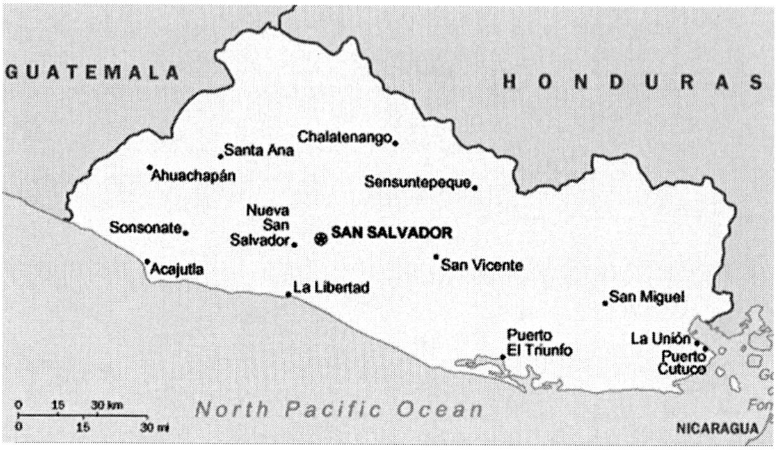

Above. Map of El Salvador.

FOREWORD TO THE NEW EDITION

This book, written with so much love, so much realism, so much honesty and so much literary beauty by my friend and comrade in the struggle, Dr Eduardo Espinoza, our beloved Felipe Dubón, is a living testimony to the great ideals that propelled the guerrilla struggle of the Farabundo Martí National Liberation Front (FMLN) in the 1980s. It is also a splendid homage to the thousands of heroes and heroines, combatants in the FMLN's military health system, who saved lives, who treated the wounded, who were psychologists even though they never studied psychology and who were an enormous bastion of morale for all our forces and for the communities that supported us in the people's war against the oligarchy and imperialism.

He skilfully captures the ingenuity, sacrifice, discipline and creativity of the health system in the FMLN, along with the small moments of simple, almost childlike happiness that heartened us in those mountains, among their vegetation and their rocks, but more than anything surrounded by the love of our comrades and the care given by our medics and doctors.

Likewise, these stories lay out for us in black and white the harsh suffering imposed by the war, which we faced with conviction and dignity, accepting decisions that needed to be taken under difficult conditions, and also accepting responsibilities that we never thought we'd be prepared to accept.

The Liberation Struggle in El Salvador: A Memoir is also a tribute to the orphaned children in our ranks, whose parents were murdered by the oligarchy's army and who had nowhere else to go than to join us. Elmer, whom I knew personally, symbolizes these small titans, who sought hope alongside us, even though they were deprived not only of toys and colouring books, but also of their home, their identity and their parents, the most basic needs of every human being.

All these stories should urge us to say together, NEVER AGAIN! Never again should oligarchic regimes be established that will build armies at their service to dominate and massacre the people. Never again should new generations face the need to take up arms to face down murderous governments.

That is what we must take charge of now, soundly building a society with social justice and democracy.

Thank you, Eduardo. When I start having doubts or when weariness sets in, when scepticism knocks at my door, I read your stories and continue the struggle.

Lorena Peña Mendoza
Former member of El Salvador's Legislative Assembly
San Salvador, 6 May 2016

FOREWORD

Dr Eduardo Espinoza has been a protagonist and a privileged witness of the revolutionary exploits that our generation experienced and that demonstrated the greatness of a large number of common women and men who were nothing less than heroes in our country. Little by little we have been learning the details of these events, thanks to works such as this little book that reconstruct our collective memory.

What the author, whose nom de guerre was Felipe Dubón, did in the revolutionary ranks and his commitment to it personifies the dreams, the integrity, the thirst for justice and the indignation that we experienced in those memorable and fateful times in our country.

The experience was filled with humanism, youthful rebelliousness channelled into grassroots struggles, dedication, solidarity, sacrifice, integrity and conviction such as I'd never seen before. Neither thirst, hunger, fatigue, exhaustion, having one's life hanging by a thread, nor the loneliness of being far from one's family kept this lot of men and women from continuing towards their objective, despite the adversity. There was never a lack of tenderness, joy, enthusiasm, optimism and the will to live.

It is time we paid a well-earned tribute to the health workers – Salvadorans and foreigners, professionals and technicians, lay healers – who gave the best of their lives without expecting anything in return. It is also right to honour the combatants – both women and men – who were wounded or lost their lives, and who were at the receiving end of this awe-inspiring medicine practised during the conflict and remembered by the author, who narrates these events and the feelings they raised with extraordinary fidelity.

These are just a few of the episodes that were experienced during that time and which need to be told, to illustrate the moral fibre of our people.

In hindsight, the organization of health services during El Salvador's civil war in the 1980s looks even more impressive and incredible: the training and wholehearted commitment of health workers in caring for combatants and civilians under such difficult conditions in the liberated zones, aided by civilian supporters, the use of appropriate technology, and a meticulous sense of how to organize the health system and care for the tools used to save lives.

The author's tales and other tales not yet told show what the people's forces are capable of when we act with a single ideal and in unity, where the common thread was the enormous conviction of triumphing over those who were opposed to establishing a regime of social justice in our country. The work isn't over yet.

Now, with his return to academia, Eduardo Espinoza – 'Felipe Dubón' in the underground – has made the journey from being a young revolutionary and warfront rebel doctor to university professor and researcher, always in the vanguard, where his concerns and aspirations are contributing to transforming our country.

Violeta Menjívar
Minister of Health of El Salvador

PREFACE AND ACKNOWLEDGEMENTS

It is hard for me to precisely categorize the experience of writing this handful of pages because it stirred up a whole gamut of contradictory feelings, some very tender, others quite painful.[1] Sorrow and joy, hope and frustration, solitude and companionship, triumph and failure mixed into the memories and this book is the product of all of this, for better or for worse.

These pages did not and do not have great aspirations. *They respond overall to my contact with young Salvadorans who have an astonishing lack of knowledge of the struggle against the military dictatorship in El Salvador, a very recent past.*

The distorted perception or ignorance in the new generations of what happened and of the context and determinants that produced the conflict is surprising. A small example: in exploring how they see those of us who got involved with the insurgent forces, I found a broad range of images that varied from a stereotypical adventurer, romantic and conspirator to a twisted personality that loves pathological violence.

Surely this is the consequence of the fact that historical memory is also terrain for political dispute. It's like reliving the history of the genocide of 1932 in El Salvador: The people tell the story one way while official accounts tell it another way. The ruling class officially declared that the grassroots leaders and heroes of the insurrection that provoked that massacre were murderers, rapists and terrorists and this is what was taught to generations for over half a century. Now we have the opportunity to assemble our memory, the memory of the people's fight against the military

[1] Adapted from: 'Presentación del libro "Relatos de la Guerra" en la Universidad de El Salvador', San Salvador, 14 August 2013.

dictatorship that oppressed the country for 50 years. But this happens because we remember and write down these events that were daily life during the war in the 1970s and 1980s, events that today seem heroic or supernatural but that were concrete events carried out by ordinary people. People, yes, who responded to what the circumstances of the moment demanded and who were brimming with nobility, solidarity and other lofty values that we are proud of, but only to the extent that we search through that historical memory to find the deep motivations that pushed them to sacrifice their lives, to give up comforts or to leave their families to dedicate themselves to a cause.

Surely I cannot justify what these positions obey, though I can explain them. For example, young people who are 20 years old now were born shortly after the Peace Accords had been signed in 1992. Likewise, the rebels with whom we lived and travelled on the volcanoes or the mountains in the territory we controlled, who left their children in the care of their mothers or their grandparents and who were fortunate enough to return, found that they were now teens or all grown up and they had to face the painful process of reconciliation and of recovering their filial love and in many cases this process went wrong because the war was a taboo subject in family conversations.

Explaining this context and the personal motivations that made each and every one of us rise up in arms is not easy.

For many, it was easier to make the decision back then than to explain today the reasons we had for doing so, because doing so was easier especially for those who joined up in the 1980s, when most joined – when open warfare had broken out between the two armies, the guerrilla army and the governmental army – than it was for those of us who joined in the 1970s.

Those of us who joined in the 1970s had to convince ourselves that to end the dictatorship there was no other choice than armed struggle and furthermore that this was not a suicidal wish or martyrdom complex, but rather that there truly was a chance for victory. So, for those who joined early on it was a much harder decision. Even so, it is very hard to explain to a young person who is living today in a totally different context, why, how and in what circumstances this decision was made, especially if that kid is one of your own children.

War is a very complex phenomenon, especially a war as long and as cruel as ours, against one of the most ferocious criminal dictatorships of our *América*.[2] Just as today political disputes occur on the field of historical memory, the war was fought on many different battlefields: in rebel-held zones where there was open combat and military manoeuvres where the two armies – the guerrilla army and the dictatorship's army – faced off; in the urban underground, against sophisticated national and international espionage experts; in the ideological field, where ideas and paradigms faced off; in the prisons and torture chambers where your conscience and ideological conviction were your only weapons; as well as in many more and complex theatres.

Today, I can proudly say that we did not neglect any of them. In all these theatres, there were heroes and heroines, most of them anonymous. Other facets of the war such as logistics and economics were so clandestine they may never see the light.

There were also abhorrent episodes of betrayal and treachery. I remember one of the most relevant cases, that of Miguel Castellanos, a member of the FPL's Political Commission, who was responsible for my ending up in jail the second time, in 1985. That time I got out in the trade for President Duarte's daughter. But that is how cruel the conflict was.

War brings out the best and the worst qualities of the human race: ambitions and the basest passions express themselves fully, as do camaraderie and solidarity. War concentrates resources and power; it breaks apart homes and families, perverts institutions and polarizes society. In short, as I said, it is very complex, it is a

[2] The Americas: Latin Americans follow a model in which all of the New World is a single continent.

history of the dead and of survivors, which ultimately is expressed in a very simple situation: the nature of facing off with your opponent in the battlefield is that you have to kill him, to avoid, in turn, being killed by him. This is a terrible decision. It involves denying your adversary the exercise of the most fundamental of all rights – the right to life. And, of course, making this decision, at least for those of us who fought with the insurgent forces, has to do with the fact that the context has characteristics that are so singular, so oppressive, so violent, so authoritarian, so exclusive, and so inequitable, that there is no other way to change it and make it fairer and more humane.

Thus, we must not lose sight of this nor enable this period to be typified simply as that of the 'civil war'. It is historically strategic to characterize the period as what is really was: *the struggle of an entire people against a military dictatorship supported by an equally greedy and criminal oligarchy.*

If I were to try to find a purpose for these stories, characterizing this period in our history would perhaps describe them the best, but characterizing it through concrete actions, experienced or carried out by real people, in that time and in those theatres of combat, that is what gives it validity. The reader can be certain that these stories are true and that just telling a few brief passages of our life in the midst of that war, without needing to add even a single milligram of fiction is what ultimately seems to me the most chilling, because I didn't have to make up anything, all I had to do was tell what happened.

That is what this book is really attempting to convey to the reader: it is not the same to say that the country was under military tyranny as it is to relate what this meant in people's daily lives, the deep imprint of the massacres, the repercussions on children's minds from seeing their parents killed and relatives tortured with great barbarity *at the hands of the legal authorities*, the tremendous anguish of families and of mothers for the fate of their children who had been kidnapped and disappeared with absolute impunity.

With these stories, I have attempted to unveil through my own experience and that of my *compañeros* how this decision and resolve gestated in the minds of the combatants and the political cadres, who with no pay, giving up everything, integrated into the very depths of their being the willingness to sacrifice the most valued of their possessions – their lives – to bequeath a better world to their children, because the one they were living in was completely unbearable.

For these same reasons, I have not delved into any political, economic or social analysis of the period, or into any of the internal disputes within the Left of that time. Individuals who were more involved and who are more authoritative than I in approaching these tasks have expressed their opinions on the matter; not with all the depth or breadth or all the forthrightness which with they should have, but there is something.

Therefore, these paragraphs try to narrate the daily activities of our guerrilla life, our torments and small joys, and above all, the context that motivated the thousands of men and women who were engaged in an effort that was so earth-shattering and so costly for the country and for many generations of Salvadorans.

Included among these are also the many internationalists who commiserated with the Salvadoran people to the extent that they each joined like one more Salvadoran and generously gave, when circumstances demanded it, of their blood and even their lives in defence of the poor and marginalized of our country, an even more valiant sacrifice because in addition to what it meant for Salvadorans to join the insurgent forces, they also had to integrate and assume other customs, other chores, different food and even a different language.

It was much harder for them and for that reason we consider them among our most beloved brethren.

Because of all this, in my conversations with combatants I liked to talk in depth with them about the story of their lives – why they were there, what had pushed them to join the rebel forces and take up arms, what had made them leave the security and warmth of home, what had been the immediate trigger leading them to devote themselves to the revolution, what made them experience joys and sorrows in those conditions of such appalling scarcity.

I never stopped being amazed, with every new story I heard, at finding a common denominator with my own life history and it was basically the sensitivity to elemental issues such as injustice, yearning for freedom, repudiation of repression and of terror as routine practices in the exercise of power, the denial of opportunities and other similar motivations.

What astonished me the most in all this was that the decision that they saw as the most natural in the world had cost me years of reading mountains of books and pamphlets in which I tried to prove to myself that there were other options besides the armed struggle to overcome the state of affairs, in which I would try to find excuses such as the fight for democracy had no chance of victory or that the military tyranny had so many strengths and such powerful allies that joining the insurgency was little more than a suicide foretold.

It was reality, that context that seems so hard for today's young folks to understand, that was responsible for showing me that it was no such thing.

For example, one of the stories herein is called 'Elmer', which tells the story of my relationship with this war orphan. Elmer carried with him the terrible events he experienced when he was perhaps seven or eight years old, so awful that it made him withdraw from relationships and he lost his speech, going completely mute for two years. It took another massive trauma, this time a shower of explosives and shrapnel during a bombing raid that he miraculously survived, for him to begin to talk again.

There were many Elmers during the war, each of them with an equal or more terrible story that is still waiting to be told. Among them, I remember a teenager at the time named Bernardo Menjívar or 'Javiercito' as we called him during the war, often using the diminutive form of his pseudonym because of his tender age. On one occasion, Javiercito blacked out during an Armed Forces air raid like the one that got Elmer to start talking again. When Javier woke up he was in the guerrilla hospital and learned that at his young 14 or 15 years both his legs had been amputated above the knee. Javier shrieked that he wanted a gun to kill himself. I don't know how he got over it, but he did and very well.

Years later, I ran into him in Nicaragua when, having surmounted his lack of formal education, he had become an electronics expert. If you didn't know his history, it was impossible to guess that he had two artificial legs. He was the leader of a rebel collective that repaired the guerrilla army's communication radios and other similar equipment. Javier now has a lovely family; he's happily married and is the father of two beautiful children. He is also doing excellent work for San Salvador's City Hall and he dedicates his meagre free time to volunteering with his fellow disabled veterans in the Dimas Rodríguez Cooperative. It was his idea that the earnings from the sale of the first edition of this book could be used to support the scholarship programme for the children of the Cooperative's war-wounded. There was no way I could refuse such a request.

Now then, knowing Javier as I did and facing the need to frequently travel abroad during the last stages of the war due to the nature of my revolutionary work, I didn't hesitate to leave my son in his care to be forged by his side and to grow up in a positive environment that would instil in him solid moral principles. I have never regretted that decision. Today I have a son of whom I am proud, who has given me an enchanting daughter-in-law and granddaughter and who is facing life with a solid set of values. These principles and values to a good extent were instilled by living and working with Javier on a daily basis, and who was like an older brother to him, for which I will never be able to thank him enough.

I also tenderly remember when I left home to go underground, which I relate here. When my mother fought to hold back her tears while she taught me to cook and to wash my clothes as the inevitable separation drew near, which I had announced to her shortly after I was released from jail. In fact, those small tasks and the things we had to forgo were certainly the hardest part of life underground. I remember that many *compañeros* who joined the guerrillas turned back, more than from fear of death or dread of combat but because they never got used to giving up the small comforts in life – cigarettes, a good drink, a clean bed and clean clothes, the warmth of home, not having to wash their own clothes, friends, hot food.... With all propriety, I can say that daily sacrifice was the anvil on which the best guerrilla fighters were forged.

Many people who have read the book have asked me whether there will be a second volume or why it is so short and say that they would have liked some 700 pages or so. Of course there is a lot to say, and some of these people have even made specific requests.

'*Look,* Compa, *since you were there when the Puente de Oro Bridge was blown up, why don't you tell the story of that battle?*'

This refers to a violent episode for control over a strategic bridge over the Lempa River, a battle we won after fighting for over twelve hours with the government troops stationed on the bridge and containing the reinforcements that the enemy was sending from the nearest barracks. The battle ended with our forces blowing up the bridge, dividing the country in two geographically on the very day the puppet president was celebrating his second anniversary in power, spoiling his party.

'*Hey* Compa *Felipe, let's get together and reminisce about how we wiped out the Fourth Brigade at the Paraíso Military Base back in December 1983.*'

This was another memorable battle in which we assembled over five hundred guerrilla fighters and our special forces in total secrecy to penetrate the last stronghold of the enemy in the depths of the territory we controlled in Chalatenango. Since I will probably write about this someday, I'll only say that three army battalions were amassed in this base along with a large group of U.S. military advisers, all Vietnam veterans, who were directly advising the government army in field operations and torture of prisoners of war, and who, among other things, mounted the security perimeter that had been built around the base, which they boasted about and which they believed made the base impregnable. They never suspected that during preparations for the obliteration of the base our special forces had already penetrated into the officers' quarters no fewer than five times. The guerrilla operation went off with amazing precision and the initial fighting left a toll of over 300 enemy forces killed and close to 150 prisoners. Battles against army reinforcements went on for over two weeks with one victory after another by our forces until the fixed government positions were completely driven out of our controlled territory.

There are also singular moments whose historical importance to our lives and to the country itself we were unable to see when they were happening or to assess in all their dimensions, such as the several times during the 1970s when I treated Salvador Cayetano Carpio ('Marcial', our first in command, who was the Army's most wanted man) and what we had to go through to remove his gall bladder in the middle of an impressive security operation in a provincial hospital, with the eyes of the entire Popular Liberation Forces (FPL) on us, watching to see what we did or did not do to their head of command. Or when I made my first contact on one of the streets of San Salvador, the capital, with the man who was my superior, who initiated me into my guerrilla adventures in a small room in a suburban rooming house. This *compañero* had enormous hands and fair skin, with a sharp and intelligent gaze, and he was a born military strategist. Over time, he and I, in addition to being comrades, forged a strong and unbreakable friendship that was interrupted by a stray bullet that never should have found him. When he died on the San Salvador volcano during the offensive of November 1989, he was the second in command of the FPL. His name was Dimas Rodríguez.

I also remember an episode with 'Elías' (Guillermo Aparicio) that I would have liked to have included. Elías was a teacher and a political operative and experienced organizer with whom I shared the rank of captain in the revolutionary army. It turns out that we both had a lot of appreciation and respect for Susana (Lorena Peña's sister), a fierce rebel, who, like the two of us, also held the rank of captain in the insurgent forces. When Susana fell in combat in Cuevitas, a town in Chalatenango, she was posthumously promoted (as had happened in other cases) to the rank of commander. This left us both somewhat resentful, because for some time Susana had earned this rank and we did not understand the reluctance to acknowledge it earlier. Because of this, in a fit of sarcasm we ended up pledging to each other that if one of us were to die in the war, the other would make sure to prevent any posthumous promotion of the one who died.

But to return to the point, I want to tell these *compañeros* and friends who ask for a sequel, that before embarking on another adventure such as this one, I need to recover from the moving experience of having written these stories, which turned out to be very painful at times.

It has been satisfying to learn that on at least three occasions this book has served to bridge the generation gap and break through a sort of mental block between parents and children because, as I already mentioned, the first returned to find the latter grown up. In these very similar cases, reading this book enabled – facilitated – breaking through that block, enabling these sons and daughters to understand the true value of the sacrifice that their parents made when they had to leave their children to fight with the guerrilla forces and to have a more accurate sense of the dimensions of this sacrifice.

For example, I remember how Laura Menéndez (a medical student whose nom de guerre was 'Lorena') would break out crying over her son, because when she joined the insurgency full time she had left him in the care of his father, who was also a progressive-thinking intellectual but who did not make the same choice that the mother of his son did. I wanted to tell that boy what his mother was like and how much she loved him. I wanted to tell him about her heroism when she died near the town of San Antonio Los Ranchos during an Army invasion when she, who had a rarely seen sense of responsibility, returned to recover the surgical equipment that had been entrusted to her and had been left behind in the confusion of the fighting in the hamlet.

Well, one day out of the blue, after I had started working as an official in the Ministry of Health, I got a phone call from Sweden, and it was this very son of Lorena's who in the randomness of life had found excerpts of my book online and had seen his mother's name in the dedication and he wanted me to tell him about her. You can imagine the emotional effect this had on me. Of course I said yes, that nothing would please me more, setting a date to talk online when I had more time. I was greatly surprised when two weeks later instead of a new call over the phone or Skype, there was Lorena's son knocking on my office door. Needless to say, we both ended up crying and hugging, overcome with emotion.

Or how I would like to tell the children of Nelly Cacao ('Mextli', another *compañera* who joined us when she was doing her social service hours before graduating) how smart and beautiful their mother was. I couldn't say if she was more beautiful than intelligent or the other way round. Her actions and thoughts overflowed with social commitment. She has the most beautiful indigenous Pipil features that I'd seen in my life, honey-coloured eyes and copper skin, all in a truly perturbing body – a combination of qualities of such a nature that there was no room left over to notice her weaknesses. She was so pretty that when she was pregnant with her second child, even when she was seven months along, she would get fiery declarations of love from the guerrilla fighters who crossed paths with her for some work reason. I would like to have the opportunity to tell these two young men that Nelly died precisely because her love for her sons, her irrepressible desire to cuddle them and convey her motherly love made her disobey security norms, and the death squads that were watching her house captured her when she returned from seeing them. Nelly was captured alive and brutally tortured, raped and mutilated before they finally killed her, but not a single word of all the strategic information she possessed passed her lips.

If I don't run into these guys beforehand, perhaps one of these days I'll dig into my reserves to find the strength to write a second part.

In conclusion, I would like to make a final appeal to the survivors of the struggle against the dictatorship and to the new generations.

To the survivors, I want to say, as we all know, that the fight against the dictatorship had a negotiated end and that the democracy that emerged from the Peace Accords is an imperfect democracy. But its imperfection has its roots in the impunity of the criminals, in the abandonment of the victims and in the still very large gaps in *our* historical memory. How can it be that we don't have a policy on memory to be able to, among many other things, make reparations and honour the victims?

For these reasons, we invite you to remember, not to return to the past, but rather to build the future. Because not only must yesterday be present today – it must also be, necessarily, part of tomorrow.

To the new generations, I also want to say that we are moving on and handing over to you the generational baton. It has been very hard to get to this point, but we feel satisfied to have pushed the wheel of time. Now there is no more war, there is no dictatorship, but there are still many inequities. It is up to you to find your way in this new context and build a more just and equitable society. And, speaking of historical memory, remember that what will be memorable tomorrow is decided and acted upon today.

I want to acknowledge the protagonists of these stories, those who are with us and those whose absence is only physical, because they are and will continue to be in our hearts and our minds.

To the *compañeros* who helped me to remember events, places and dates.

To David Hernández, who encouraged me to write ad nauseam.

To Pablo Benítez, who reviewed the style and made valuable suggestions about the manuscript.

To Laura Zavaleta, assistant to Dr David Hernández, who also carefully reviewed the manuscript.

To Luis Lindo, Alberto Bertulazzi and Ramón 'El Suizo' who provided me with the photographs.

To Elena Rodas, who did the beautiful design and layout of the original Spanish edition, as well as the poster and invitation to the book launching at the University of El Salvador.

To Violeta, dear and beloved *compañera* in the struggle, who took the time to write such a warm foreword despite her commitments.

To Wilfredo Zepeda, always fraternal, supportive and generous, who accompanied me in this adventure with his formidable ideological clarity, political sharpness and sagacity, surpassed only by his modesty.

To my family, especially my mother, who are my everyday heroes and without whose affection and support I surely would not be here today.

Eduardo Espinoza ('Felipe Dubón')
14 August 2013

I see those who in any land have died for the good cause;
The seed is spare, nevertheless the crop shall never run out;
(Mind you O foreign kings, O priests, the crop shall never run out.)
– Walt Whitman, from 'Song of the Broad-Axe'

INTRODUCTION

In the 1970s and 1980s, El Salvador lived through one of the most important periods in its history. However the origins and trajectory of the social upheaval that shook the country are analysed, its participants were protagonists of an epic feat and we are all responsible for its narrative. To remain silent would be to disrespect our homeland and the blood spilled by the best of its progeny. Today's generations and those to come merit more than a simple accounting of the wounded, disabled, deceased and disappeared.

My perspective and my involvement are from the side of the insurgent forces and could probably appear biased or exaggerated to some. However, after rereading these accounts, I am left with a sensation of superficiality or partiality from not being capable of or knowing how to touch more deeply on the generations of suffering and silent heroism of the humble people, who, with their example and solidarity, inspired our devotion to the worthy cause of a better future.

I joined the *Fuerzas Populares de Liberación 'Farabundo Martí'* (FPL) in 1975, one week after I was an eyewitness to the massacre of the unarmed and peaceful student demonstration of July 30th, which was protesting human rights violations by repressive government security forces. Until that point, the fear of being arrested, the fear of torture, the fear of death and all the other forms that terror took in those days, kept me from going further than sporadically and fearfully treating a patient or teaching a couple of first-aid classes. But on 30 July, the rage, the impotence and the crack of rifle butts against our bodies overcame my fear as my classmate Francisco Escobar and I were attacked by the National

Guard when we attempted to get some of the wounded to safety.

Readers who did not live through the war in El Salvador will most likely find it very difficult to imagine the situation that forced many of us to take up arms and these chronicles are not meant to do so, although they may help some. Rather they are meant to tell a few 'war stories'. However, the contact I have had as a professor with many young people provides the impetus for this introduction. The war was not something desirable, nor the fruit of an adventurous spirit, nor a romantic episode. We committed all our will and our strength to changing an unbearable and unsustainable state of affairs.

We were living with a wretched and violent military tyranny, an absolute lack of democracy, a total disregard for human life and boundless abuse of the people. Friends and acquaintances were arrested and disappeared on a daily basis, while the corruption and arrogance of the military establishment constantly affronted our dignity. Every day, awareness of this reality and the need to organize seeped in through all our senses. Nowhere in the country could you walk for more than a block without running into soldiers, National Guard, National Police, Treasury Police, rural paramilitary patrols, civil defence, *Orden* (a death squad), the secret police and other forces. One in every five Salvadorans belonged, by force or by choice, to one of these repressive forces, which schooled their members in betrayal, torture and death. There was only one thing between being true to this subcutaneous awareness and opposing all of this and joining the armed insurgence: fear (or its counterpart: bravery).

As I said, my fear became history on 30 July 1975. From then on, I steeled myself and increasingly devoted myself 'to the struggle'. I cared for the wounded, I taught combatants first aid, I designed advanced health courses, I trained for the physical rigours of war, I recruited colleagues and organized them into support collectives, and I read piles of books and broadsides on wars of liberation, Marxism, sociology, history, conspiratorial methods and everything and anything I could get my hands on. This was the time of the development of the urban guerrilla forces, a premonitory period characterized by strict rules for clandestine operations and compartmentalization for survival.

At the same time, we were helping to build, working in health care, the most powerful and daring mass movement (*las masas*) ever seen in Latin America, which would become our rear guard, our mountain, our inexhaustible breeding ground.

In 1981, this uncontainable build-up of forces, spurred by an increase in repression, made a qualitative leap and burst out into open confrontation between two armies: the government and the insurgency. Organizational and preparatory considerations related to the looming fight, led me to transfer in December 1980 to the Chinchontepec Volcano, where I was tasked with organizing the medical and hospital services of the FPL in the José Roberto Sibrián Paracentral Front, the second-largest concentration of guerrilla forces of this political-military organization after the Chalatenango Department.

The rebels' military health system was a strategic factor for troop morale and keeping them in shape to fight, as well as for taking care of the thousands of civilians living in the large rebel-controlled zones where government services were no longer being provided.

Specifically, and just as the other stories, the chapter titled 'Rebel Hospital' tells an authentic experience, meticulously true, that brings to light many aspects of the political and technical work we did in rebel-held territory – organizing health services by levels of complexity, logistical supply to the hospitals, appropriate technology, training local human resources and transporting the wounded, plus other jobs – that shows how all these elements became stretched to the limit in an extreme situation, such as many that we would experience throughout the civil war in El Salvador.

Of course, the health work wasn't done exclusively by the health workers at the front lines. Behind them, with decided support and in close relationship (this story is not told in this book), was a powerful and thriving community organization that was given the most varied names and would change its facade and structure, evincing infinite creativity. This broad network of citizens from all walks of life and occupations included humble health workers, auxiliary and graduate nurses in almost all the country's health facilities, clinical laboratory technicians, anaesthetists, physical therapists, dentists, internists, psychologists, surgeons from a wide array of specializations and general practitioners, etc. On the job, sheltering the wounded in their homes, performing valuable tests, making dressings and bandages, and carrying out hundreds of much smaller tasks, they supplemented the work of those who were at the front lines and of the communities, who, armed with nothing more than their organization and their faith in the revolutionary process, made the sustained and growing advance of this process possible.

The course of the war and the particular circumstances of the conflict meant that occasionally I would have to engage in work that took me away from my medical practice. However, I never could really let it go completely and I returned to medicine full time after the Peace Accords were signed.

These other tasks I performed also left an indelible mark as deep as the health work. This experience is partially described in 'Elmer', the story of my relationship with a war orphan who grew up and became a man by my side in the midst of that bloody conflict.

I hope that this narrative about a transcendental period in our country will motivate other protagonists and witnesses to also tell their own stories for the new generations.

Let's see then, the events . . .

ARCHBISHOP ROMERO – *MONSEÑOR*

Other prelates need a surname to be identified, but every Salvadoran knows Archbishop Oscar Arnulfo Romero simply as '*Monseñor*'[1] and no one, believer or non-believer, gets confused or mistakes this moniker for someone else. Anyone who visits his tomb in San Salvador's Metropolitan Cathedral will never find it deserted. A perpetual parade of people, mostly of humble origins, visit it every day, murmuring a prayer and lighting a candle. 'It's for a miracle he did for me,' a woman with a child in arms told me once, when she realized I was watching her curiously, while another child just barely bigger hung onto her skirts and her grimy apron.

Christians in other latitudes call this humble Salvadoran 'Saint Romero of the Americas'.

I met him in the parish of Aguilares in 1976 while teaching first aid to farmers of the Christian Federation of Salvadoran Farmers (FECCAS) and the Rural Workers' Union (UTC). Another priest introduced us, who would also be assassinated: Rutilio Grande. After that, I saw him on various occasions, always in the parishes of Aguilares or El Paisnal and almost always with Father Rutilio. The two of them had a lovely, close friendship and several times they took advantage of my presence in a course to ask me to examine a sick parishioner. Sometimes they would come to my talks. I remember one instance how they laughed as I showed several lay midwives how to deliver a baby, when, helped by two of the midwives, I improvised to illustrate my explanations with a watermelon for the foetus and a rolled up towel as the birth canal.

[1] The Archbishop Romero Trust: http://www.romerotrust.org.uk/.

Monseñor always transformed the ambience. His speech was spontaneous, sincere and deep, while at the same time simple. When we were all sweating fear, his presence emanated respect, trust and serenity. Listening to him back then, I understood why, when he was preaching his Sunday sermon, the streets in *every* town, including the capital, would be deserted and in every home the radio would be tuned to YSAX, the archbishopric's radio station, to hear his clear, direct and simple voice. It was a voice of censure, committed to the meek, 'The Voice of the Voiceless', the voice the powers to be wanted to silence but which continues and will continue to be the message of hope and redemption of the poor.

I saw him again in 1978. He didn't strike me as a miracle-making saint or a supernatural being then, either. He was still the same fair, sincere and simple man who made you feel really good. His presence continued to convey the same sensation of peace and tranquillity. I had gone to see him to thank him for contributing, from his pulpit,[2] to my liberation, by demanding respect for my life and liberty after the army had captured me at the door to the Colonia Guatemala church, on the last day of the novena following my father's death. I was kept disappeared and tortured for two months. When officials, military officers and even friends closed the door in the face of my elderly mother, who was desperately looking for me, he consoled her and kept her hope alive. This was surely a small miracle.

Three circumstances came together beyond chance to make my release possible: The third and definitive one was the intercession of *Monseñor*. Before that, the first was the final match in the football World Cup between Argentina and the Netherlands. That day, my torturers did not accompany, as was their habit, the

[2] Oscar A. Romero, Homily of Sunday 9 July 1978 (p. 49) and homily of Sunday 23 July 1978 (p. 89), in *Monseñor Oscar A. Romero: Su Pensamiento V. Colección Homilías y Diario de Mons*, 2nd ed., San Salvador: Publicaciones Pastorales del Arzobispado and Imprenta Criterio, March 2000.

common prisoner who would, once a day, distribute a shapeless, rancid mass of rice and beans between two tortillas (which they called a 'yoyo'). They preferred to watch Diego Maradona's moves during the final. The second circumstance was the prisoner who was handing out the yoyos, who, seeing me naked on the floor of my narrow cell, full of bruises from the previous night's beating, pressed up against the bars that separated me from the hallway and said:

'They really gave it to you last night, didn't they buddy?'

'Yep,' I replied, 'every night they beat me.'

'And at home do they know that you're here?'

'I don't think so,' I told him.

'Well, ya' know, I get out tomorrow. My 30 days are up and if you want, I could take them a note.'

'I'm naked and have nothing,' I told him distressed.

'Hang on. I'll be right back with something to write with.'

A couple of minutes later, which felt like centuries, he reappeared with a crumpled foil wrapper from a pack of cigarettes and a ballpoint pen that had seen much better days. While I hurriedly explained how to get to my house, I wrote on the scrap as best I could:

> My name is Eduardo Espinoza. I'm a doctor. My identity card number is XXXXX and I'm detained, incommunicado, and being tortured in the basement of the National Police for political reasons.

That humble citizen and Good Samaritan, sentenced to serve my torturers for 30 days because of his drinking, risked his life hiding the note in his rectum, took it out of the dungeons and got it to my mother, who visited *Monseñor* again with that proof of my arrest and, up until then, disappearance by my tormentors. *Monseñor*'s courageous public denunciation and his private advocacy before officials and human rights defence agencies with that crumpled bit of paper, forced my captors to transfer me to the remand prison in Santa Tecla – which is now a museum – and bring me before the court.

After giving my statement, I demanded, through a lawyer provided by the Archbishopric's legal aid office, *Socorro Jurídico*, also founded by *Monseñor*, a handwriting test to demonstrate that my signature was not the one on the 'extrajudicial statement' that was sufficient evidence to prosecute and sentence 'subversives' according to the Law for the Guarantee and Defence of Public Order in effect at that time. When I requested the expert opinion, the government withdrew the charges and the statement and two days later they declared me free 'for lack of evidence'. Several days later, after being harassed at home and work and being constantly followed and threatened, I joined the FPL full time as a medical collaborator with the guerrillas.

After that, a rush of events took over. I was being politically persecuted and had no public life, and therefore, could no longer meet with *Monseñor*. When he was assassinated, on 24 March 1980, I couldn't contain my rage and sadness. Because of that, even though my organization forbade us from attending his funeral for security reasons, I went to his interment anyway, to his mass, to the multitudinous farewell he was given by 'the voiceless'. And perhaps that was another small miracle. After all, I owed it to him; he had demanded my freedom without fear or conditions.

During the funeral mass celebrated from the cathedral portico, snipers on the nearby National Palace and other government buildings sowed panic and death among the multitude in the plaza. In the midst of the maelstrom, I ended up being swept by a human tide into the cathedral basement. Outside, 'the voiceless' were generously donating their blood to recover and guard the mortal remains of their Pastor, which were inhumed in the same cathedral where he made history and where they say that he makes miracles today and which is why he should be canonized. I don't know if he will be canonized eventually, nor do I think he would have cared; if someone would have told him while he was alive, he would have certainly laughed, incredulous.

I've always been sceptical of miracles and such, which is why I've never asked for a miracle. However (after all, I owe him my freedom and my life), once in a while I visit his tomb and when I'm there, his memory moves me to tears and afterwards floods me with peace and tranquillity.

It's as though he were alive.

THE FAREWELL, OR, AN OCTOBER AFTERNOON IN 1978

Mother and Son

'*Mamá*, I've connected with the *compañeros* and we've talked several times since I got out of jail. I told them I only have two options: either I leave the country or I join them in the underground movement. Yesterday they told me everything was ready, so next week I'm leaving to join the guerrillas full time. It's safer for everyone. If I stay here and continue working at the National University, the death squads will end up killing me or doing something to the family.'

'Wouldn't it be better if you left the country, son? Your Aunt Berta says that if you go to Honduras she can guarantee you a position in the Ministry of Health and work in her husband's hospital in Santa Rosa or in Tegucigalpa. Or you could accept the graduate school scholarship the National University is offering you or the offer from Father Guillermo when he came to see you and suggested you to go to Ohio, that they would help you with the asylum application and your medical residency. . . . It's been just four months since your father died and if something happens to you I think I'll die.'

'I'm not going to run away, that's not the way the two of you raised me. I have to fight for what I believe in. That was always my father's example.'

(She sobs quietly.)

'*Mamá*, don't make it harder for me, give me courage, have faith in me.'

(Saying no more, she retires to her room.)

The Next Day

'Son. . .'

'Yes?'

(With tears in her eyes.) 'And who is going to cook for you there?'

'We'll do it, *Mamá*. We'll share all the chores. We'll take turns.'

'And do you know how to cook?'

'Uh, no. But I'll learn.'

'Come, I'm going to show you how to make steak and rice. Everything else is just a variation on that.'

Epilogue

Three days later, after passing muster under the loving gaze and instructions of my mother's crash course in cooking and in how to hand-wash and iron shirts and pants, I left home bound for the underground. My mother blessed me, she hugged me and she sent me on my way with a kiss and a forced smile for which I silently thanked her. I remember the expression on her face – an odd mix of motherly anguish and pride in my decision.

REBEL HOSPITAL

On 2 June 1982, while I was on my way back to the Barrios plantation, on the side of Chinchontepec volcano, where our field hospital was, I was thinking about how much the health care structure had evolved. At this point in the conflict all of the war zones – North, Central, Paracentral, etc. – had an '*Hospital del Frente*' where we had the most qualified technicians and the most wholehearted, devoted and capable clinicians.

During the three hour walk, my courier Pedro, a 12-year-old kid, was happily chatting with Walter, the *compañero* who usually accompanied me along the volcano's trails. At that time I was in charge of health for the Paracentral Front and the command required that I always have someone with me for security. I hung back a little on purpose so that my companions' conversation wouldn't interfere with my musings. A year and a half of open war had taught us a lot about what types of care were needed and how to distribute the different levels of care within the war zone and how and on what subjects to train the people who ran the services.

The situation was notably different from the medical care delivered during the previous decade, when services were provided to a basically urban guerrilla force. At that time, conspiratorial methods prevailed. Clandestine hospitals with apparently normal middle-class facades would be located in a neighbourhood like any other. Likewise, the ambulances were covert, transporting staff and patients who would wear sunglasses with the lenses carefully covered in opaque tape to keep them from recognizing the route to the hospital. The patients and the medical staff all covered their heads with hoods in these undercover locations so they wouldn't recognize each other and couldn't identify each other later on in the street, at school or in another hospital. They worked under strict rules of compartmentalization, with codes and pseudonyms, and psychological preparation against probable arrests and the inevitable torture; the whole nine yards.

While evoking all this, I remembered the first day I entered the Chinchontepec volcano zone (the '*volcancito*' as we would later take to calling it affectionately when we had to leave it apprehensively for some task or when we would return safe and sound to its secure and inviting ravines). Together with 'Nena' (Carmen Paniagua, a graduate nurse), we'd been picked up in San Marcos by the lorry that transported grain to the guerrillas. It was 27 December 1980. We crossed the town of Zacatecoluca and headed up the road to San Vicente. We had left a government army roadblock and checkpoint some 20 minutes earlier when Toribio, the driver, said that our contact was about 50 metres up the road.

The rebel troops were waiting for us. It only took 15 minutes to unload the lorry, which was packed full, with us perched on top of the sacks. We shook hands with Toribio and almost without realizing it we were in the middle of the column at two in the afternoon under a scorching sun, commencing our climb to Paz Opico, the guerrilla encampment where the General Staff of the Paracentral Front was based. When Nena and I arrived an hour later, the rest of the column, each of them loaded with a hundred-pound sack, had already been there for at least 20 minutes. We found them resting as they enjoyed making fun of how exhausted and dishevelled we looked.

When I asked where the hospital was, they pointed me to the local church, and as I walked towards it, Sonia[1] and her partner Pedro[2] came out to greet me. They had been in the FMLN for almost six months. In addition to being their physiology professor

[1] Dr Isis Dagmar Pocasange, who died on 18 April 1992 of breast cancer.

[2] Dr Carlos Linares, captured alive, tortured and killed in Cerro Colorado, Cinquera in 1989 by the government army, alongside Jurg Weiss, a Swiss member of the European Parliament.

back in medical school, I had also been their connection for political activities years later in San Salvador and they were very excited by my arrival. They thought that my organizing experience would be very helpful in the war zone and while I was taking off my backpack, they launched headlong into telling me about dozens of experiences, problems and the needs facing them. That night I slept like a blessed baby at the foot of the altar in the Paz Opico church, which housed the rebel hospital. The next morning at 7:00 AM, I was in the foyer at Los Cocos Plantation, about 15 minutes from Paz Opico, waiting to be seen by *compañero* Luis, better known as Luisón,[3] the commander of the Paracentral Front.

'Come in, Felipe. (No one there used their real names, except a few of the locals, and Felipe was my nom de guerre.) I was told you'd arrived yesterday and I was expecting you.'

'Yes,' I answered, 'I've been talking with Pedro, Sonia and Carlos Barbón,[4] and I want to start working as soon as possible, so I've come so you can tell me what I'll be doing.'

'Don't overthink it,' he said while pointing at a map. 'As of today, you're in charge of health care for the front that covers the volcano; the zone from San Jacinto that runs between the road to Tecoluca, the Pan-American Highway, the Coastal Highway and the Lempa River; and the coastal zone that goes from the Coastal Highway to the Pacific Ocean. The health organization in the zones that we control in the east are also under your responsibility, meaning northern San Miguel and the part of Usulután that borders on the Lempa River north of the Coastal Highway. You have two weeks to do an inventory of human resources and submit your work plan.'

He paused, lit a cigarette and continued:

'Your immediate superior will be Miguel Tijerilla. He is the

[3] Juan Méndez, ex-sergeant of the governmental army and member of the Central Command of the FPL.

[4] Our anaesthetist, who earned his nickname for his bushy beard. I would enjoy our conversations by starlight, especially because of his exquisite sense of black humour.

head of services at the front and a member of my military staff and in addition to health, he is also in charge of supplies and logistics. One thing – he doesn't like to be called Tijerilla. Any questions?'

Of course I had a million questions, but I couldn't say a word, dazed by everything I'd just heard. I'd better just ask my staff and that Tijerilla for details before I say something foolish, I thought to myself.

'I think everything's clear, although I can't see all the details yet. I'll begin right away by surveying the terrain and meeting folks and in one week I'll send you a preliminary report with my assessment and needs. I'm looking forward to working with you,' I said as I extended my hand.

'Okay. I'll be waiting to hear from you,' he answered.

I sensed some unease when he shook my hand, but didn't pay much attention to it as I turned and began to walk out. But as I was crossing the threshold, I heard him call me.

'Felipe . . .'

'Yes? . . .'

'This is a military structure and it is our army in formation. You must learn to salute your superiors, to ask permission to speak and also to leave. You have to demand the same from your subordinates. This is known as military courtesy and along with other rules that you'll learn in due time, it is essential for discipline. This is not like the city; you have to learn to take refuge and to camouflage yourself, to defend yourself from air raids and avoid being ambushed. Tell Miguel to sign you up for a course for combatants because you never know. The enemy doesn't respect hospitals or medical workers or anything and it's better to be prepared. You'll need a weapon, a side-arm of course, since we don't have enough long-arms for the combatants. I'll send it to you in a couple of days.'

The gun in question took almost a month to arrive, and while I was walking up to Barrios, I patted it at my side. It was a silver .357 Magnum revolver with mother-of-pearl grips and by this time I'd shot it several times to test my aim and get used to it, since my life could depend on how good a shot I was.

A blast in the distance down by the highway, followed by several bursts of rifle fire, jerked me out of my reverie and brought me back to the present. It was a land mine.

Time and the war had educated my ear and almost without realizing it, I had learned to distinguish the blast of a 60 mm mortar shell from that of an 81 mm one, a grenade launched by a Chinese RPG-2 rocket-launcher from one shot from a 90 mm cannon, a hand grenade from an M-79 grenade-launcher, and of course the already classic '*minazo*' – the explosion caused by a military vehicle driving over a guerrilla land mine. This simple yet effective home-made explosive device was made from ammonium nitrate (commonly used to fertilize the coffee groves) and aluminium powder. Panicked soldiers called it the 'Death Ray' and they were right.

Walter turned around and looked at me with a big grin; he was 16 years old, full of enthusiasm and yearned for combat.

'*Compa* Felipe! Did you hear that? It was an ambush. I saw when the squad from La India camp went out to set up. I'll bet they were waiting about eight hours out there for the enemy. Three-fingered Hugo was in command; he wouldn't miss a *minazo*. It must have taken out at least ten men. You'll see when we get back.'

I went back to my thoughts, since I had more than enough on my mind. The reason for my visit to Barrios was to review preparations, given that an invasion of the volcano by government troops was imminent. The army had been amassing troops in San Vicente and Zacatecoluca for several days and had moved pieces of artillery to the Jiboa sugar mill and increased their patrols and roadblocks on nearby roads. Plus, intelligence reports confirmed the speculation and observations about the invasion in question. What worried me most was the extent of the army's preparedness and number of troops. This was not normal for a routine incursion into our controlled zones and it gave me a bad feeling.

The health command and a small field hospital run by Nacho[5] were still in Paz Opico, but the main *Hospital del Frente* had been moved to Barrios, because the wounded, health facilities, and in particular, the medical and paramedical staff were particularly coveted military objectives. This situation forced us to arm ourselves, to remain hidden in the depths of the controlled zones and to camouflage the facilities rather than identify them. The conditions in Barrios couldn't have been better for this purpose. Its location between two mountain spurs made it unreachable by artillery fire, unless the weapons were located in a rebel-held zone, which would be quite difficult, but not impossible, as I would soon find out. The only possibility would be an airstrike, but it would take exceptional skill to drop the bombs in between the spurs and then pull up quickly to avoid crashing into the sides of the volcano. Plus, around three in the afternoon a thick fog would usually roll in and cover the plantation.

'Here comes the anti-air defence!' the patients and the

[5] Dr Tomás Chávez, a Mexican physician who joined the Paracentral Front in 1981.

sanitarios[6] would say.

In Barrios, I was met by Carlos Barbón[7] and René.[8] I quickly brought them up to date on the latest reports on the invasion.

After lunch, we began to systematically review the work that had been done. All the directives and orders we'd sent had been scrupulously followed. The chronic patients were evacuated to communities outside the zone, the supply of hammocks and stretchers was fortified and alcohol production stepped up. All the first-aid kits for the combat-unit *sanitarios* were restocked with materials that had been recently sterilized (in traditional mud-brick bread ovens). An enormous amount of first-aid materials were prepared: gauze, compresses, swabs, dressings, etc. We built up the supply of intravenous fluids, antibiotics and anaesthetics (particularly ketamine). All the materials were divided into lots that contained a little of everything and were spread among different *tatús*[9] in different spots on the volcano, to make sure they would be available no matter which zone we would end up in.

Responsibility for safekeeping of the minor-surgery[10] and laparotomy[11] sets, particularly valuable to our work, had been delegated to the most trustworthy *compañeros* and everyone was working feverishly to tie up all the loose ends.

'How many soldiers are coming?' asked René the next day while I was getting ready to return to Paz Opico.

[6] Medics.

[7] Rolando Alvarenga, psychology student and later anaesthetist, trained in our underground metropolitan hospitals.

[8] Dr Eduardo Coto, obstetric-gynaecologic surgeon until 1980 and later the best and most skilful general surgeon I have ever known.

[9] Concealed subterranean shelters and tunnels built by guerrilla forces to house and protect provisions, medicines, weapons, supplies and wounded combatants.

[10] Minor-surgery set: Instruments used for minor interventions such as suturing and dressing wounds, etc.

[11] Laparotomy set: Surgical instruments used to open the abdominal cavity and repair injuries in cases of perforating abdominal wounds or other diseases or circumstances requiring opening the abdomen.

'We don't know for sure, but no fewer than ten thousand. It's the most we've seen so far. The *compas* are very optimistic and are preparing for the showdown but I think we need to anticipate a considerable number of casualties, perhaps fifty in the initial battles during the first two weeks,' I told him.

'Two weeks! I don't think it will last that long,' René responded. 'It'll be like always, at the end of the first week they'll leave with their tails between their legs and heavy losses and we'll just have a couple of minor wounds to deal with.'

'Let's hope so, but we also need to keep our guard up.'

Two days later the fighting began.

Surgery Under Fire

The newly formed Atlacatl Battalion, trained by U.S. advisers in anti-guerrilla tactics, was making its debut.

They would provide a taste of their practical and bloodthirsty lessons barely a week later at Hacienda Peñas, located on the slopes of the volcano. A group of old folks, women and children from a Protestant sect remained there, refusing to flee despite the repeated pleas by mass movement leaders and guerrilla military leaders for them to retreat under our protection. They trusted the government army to respect them because of their religious beliefs. But when the soldiers arrived at the centre of the hacienda, they surrounded the villagers, forced them outside and after pushing the confused crowd into the courtyard, machine-gunned them down mercilessly. In Barrios, we heard the shooting that day and figured it was a battle, though we thought it odd not to hear grenades. Shortly thereafter, we found out about the massacre.

The Atlacatl Battalion was backed up by thousands of additional soldiers from the Fifth Brigade in San Vicente, the base in Usulután and CIIFA (Armed Forces Engineer Instruction Centre) in Zacatecoluca, in addition to two battalions brought in from the Second Brigade in Santa Ana and several hundred more

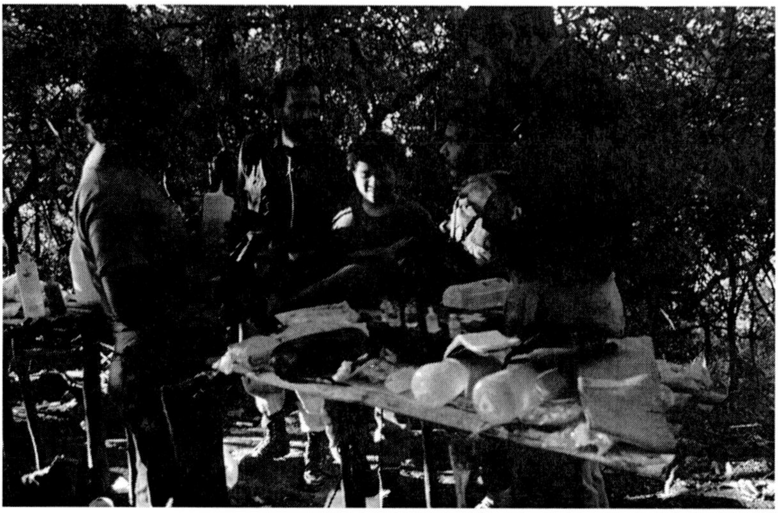

troops from the Sensuntepeque barracks.

Artillery support came from the cavalry regiment and, together with air support, formed the largest mobilization of enemy troops ever seen. The idea was for the Atlacatl Battalion to victoriously begin the woeful and controversial role it would play throughout the war.

Two weeks later, the fighting continued just as fierce as it was at the beginning. The government army continued to advance despite suffering considerable casualties, and our hospital was receiving an average of three wounded a day transferred from field hospitals.

The lack of sleep and fatigue began to wear on the rebel fighters and food became scarce. Paz Opico had already been abandoned and taken by the enemy and in Barrios we could hear the mortar and rifle fire coming more or less from a steep slope known as Cuesta del Mono (halfway between Paz Opico and Barrios).

I had arrived to reinforce the hospital staff a week earlier and we had already spent three days and nights working ceaselessly. René and I were the only surgeons. A couple of days earlier, Nacho, who had also come to work in the hospital as a reinforcement, had been sent outside the area of the military operation with a column of some thirty people with minor injuries and some seven 'hammock cases'. This was done to lighten the load on the hospital structure, since the unbending advance of the government troops did not presage anything good. Nacho left reluctantly since he wanted to remain in the combat zone. But someone had to leave with the column of wounded and also set things up to receive patients and health personnel in the event that it became impossible to hold positions on the volcano. We leaned toward having Nacho be the one to accompany the wounded, because, not long before, in November 1981, in combat against troops from the Third Brigade, he'd been wounded by a 120 mm mortar shell that also killed his partner Lupita.[12] Nacho's wound had injured his sciatic nerve, leaving him with a limp and making it difficult for him to walk quickly, which could be dangerous in the event that, as we were expecting, the fighting escalated. We also made Federico[13] join the column of wounded that we were evacuating. Neither René nor I had clean clothes and we were spattered with blood from head to toe.

At ten o'clock at night our waiting list included a gunshot wound to the abdomen, an unconscious *compa* with cerebral oedema from the expansion wave of a 500 pound bomb dropped by a plane, and another *compañero* in the middle of having his right arm amputated, which had been almost completely destroyed by a grenade from an M-79 launcher. I applied a tourniquet made from a blood pressure cuff to this last patient and injected him with an ampoule of morphine. He was as white as a sheet.

'Is anyone related to this *compa*?' I shouted to be heard above

[12] Estela Benítez, originally from Mexico, died when she was destroyed by the same 120 mm mortar shell that wounded Nacho on the slopes of Chinchontepec Volcano.

[13] Fred van der Ven, a Dutch physician who came to collaborate with the guerrillas 'for three months' and who stayed with us for four years. We had to force him to leave because his family raised a huge fuss claiming that we had been holding him against his will.

the tremendous din.

'Me! I'm his brother!' a tall, husky rebel fighter answered.

'I need your blood,' I told him, 'or he won't survive the anaesthesia or the operation. What's your blood type? Do you know your brother's blood type?'

'No . . . I don't know, *Compa*.'

'What do you mean you don't know? We typed everyone exactly for these cases! How can you not know? Don't you realize that your brother is dying? What are you thinking? You think we do miracles? What a crock . . .'

I was really furious and I gave in to all my exhaustion, exploding in anger. The hardened *guerrillero*'s eyes misted and he said in a broken voice:

'Forgive me, *Compa*, I'm from the FAL and we don't have a doctor there. I carried him here by myself from the front lines so no more *compas* would stop fighting, but the truth is that I don't know anything about blood types.'

When he said that, I was mortified. The FAL, the armed wing of the Communist Party, had a unit to the north-west of the volcano and it was true that they didn't have medical support for their combatants. Despite being a relatively small unit, they had mounted a line of fire, which they had shrewdly combined with several ambushes, keeping the enemy from advancing thus far. If it weren't for them, the hospital would have had to retreat much earlier.

'Listen, please forgive me,' I said. 'I am so tired that I don't even know what I'm saying. Look, in any case, I'm going to need you to give blood to your brother because you're the only candidate that we can be sure won't cause a reaction. We'll save ourselves the typing and we'll give it to him.'

In truth, we had run out of typing sera, so we had no way of knowing the blood type of any of them. I did a rudimentary cross-matching test (which I'd seen my father, also a physician, do when I was in high school in La Unión) mixing two drops of blood on a glass slide. If the blood didn't clump, I would know that the chances of a rejection reaction would be minimal; because they were brothers, they should have a similar genetic makeup. I waited a moment and then put the slide under the microscope, whose only working objective was 10x. As I expected, there was no apparent incompatibility reaction, so I drew blood from him and transfused it into his wounded brother.

While I was supervising the transfusion and René was administering IV steroids to Eulises (the cerebral oedema patient), a dispatch arrive from Juan, the commander of the front at the time. Juan had replaced Luisón, who had fallen in combat along with Silvia,[14] one of our most valuable *compañeras*, during an overpowering battle on the coast of San Vicente. I broke the seal and began to read: '. . . the FAL can no longer hold their position and will retreat tonight. They will evacuate all their units from the volcano. This means that Barrios will be unprotected on the northwest flank. Station advance sentinels and prepare to evacuate the hospital. [. . .] I'll send you a squad first thing in the morning to provide security while you retreat by the agreed route.'

The night wore on. I was drinking a cup of coffee when René came over to me.

'I think Rebequita is going into labour,' he started. 'I'm worried. The baby's head hasn't engaged and her blood pressure is rising. If things go on like this, she'll need a C-section.'

'A C-section! Son-of-a-bitch! Just what we need – a C-section!'

Rebequita was a *compañera* who worked in the explosives workshop and was in charge of making nitrate,[15] a basic component

[14] Ana Vilma Miranda, a physician who was captured alive in a battle in Hacienda La Sabana, in the lower reaches of the Lempa River in San Vicente. She was summarily executed along with other survivors.

[15] Ammonium nitrate: A fertilizer widely used in coffee fields and which the people in their wisdom had rapidly incorporated into their armamentarium. When the enemy realized how widely it was being used and to what effect, it stopped its importation and manufacture, but the guerrillas figured out how to obtain nitric acid and ammonia and to set up their own factories in the

of grenades, of mines used in ambushes and of antitank bombs detonated against armoured vehicles, which were made of a base of nitric acid and ammonium using a delicate and dangerous process of mixing these substances. Her partner was none other than Miguel Tijerilla, my immediate boss, who was constantly the target of my jokes about the way Rebequita would always manage to get her way in arguments with him, skilfully disarming him despite the fact that his ingenuity and mischief were famous throughout the FMLN.

I tried to calm down and answered René.

'Look, we still have to do a laparotomy and the amputation for the *compa* from the FAL. Let's get that done first and in the meantime, have a *compa* monitor the foetal heart and the labour. I hope a C-section won't be necessary. In any case, we'll do it in the early morning, when the picture is clearer and we're sure it's the only option.'

'Uh . . . Okay. But I think it will end up being a C-section.'

The abdominal surgery and the amputation took almost our entire night. We finished at four-thirty in the morning and dropping from exhaustion on the veranda of the house, fell asleep haphazardly on the floor. At six in the morning we were awoken by several rounds of rifle fire that sounded no more than an hour away.

'Rebequita!' René and I exclaimed, in unison, and we ran inside.

When we arrived, she was clearly in labour, but her cervix was not dilating, her blood pressure was 160/110, her legs were swollen and the foetal heart rate was dangerously elevated, indicating foetal distress.

'We can't wait any longer,' René said. 'She has pre-eclampsia[16]

rear guard zones.

[16] Disorder of pregnancy, characterized by hypertension and swelling of the lower limbs. Emergency termination of the pregnancy via caesarean section is indicated to prevent seizures and maternal or foetal death.

and we have to go in now. And with all that firing so close we don't know what conditions will be like later.'

'Let's go,' I said. 'I'll tell Carlos to give her an epidural.'

I was frankly alarmed by the nearby fighting and I'd told Nena and the rest of the staff to prepare to evacuate the patients and head to Palmo Chacho (the next stop on our planned escape route) and for the patients who could walk and the *sanitarios* carrying surgical supplies to begin the march. Old Man Simón, then head of hospital services, and his sons Eliseo and Toño, were organizing the hammock-bearers for patients who couldn't walk on their own.

Epidural anaesthesia is plainly contraindicated with blood pressure this high, but we couldn't even imagine having nitrous oxide (laughing gas) and oxygen, since we didn't have the necessary equipment for inhalation analgesia, and we had run out of ketamine a long time ago.

Carlos skilfully inserted the needle in the spinal canal and administered the regional anaesthetic. In a few minutes, Rebequita was lying on her back and the lower half of her body was numb. Carlos was trying to calm her down and reassure her by talking to her softly and distracting her.

'There's only one pair of gloves left,' René told me in a pained tone.

'You wear them,' I said. 'I'm going to apply Merthiolate after washing.'

The spinal anaesthesia had taken effect and we began the surgery. René operated while I assisted and acted as scrub nurse at the same time, and Mayra, a sharp *campesina*,[17] did the job of circulating nurse.[18] With a sure, steady hand René made a deep infraumbilical incision and just as I began to clamp the bleeding

[17] Rural peasant farmer or farm-worker.

[18] In the operating theatre, everyone who is present during surgery has a defined role: surgeon (René), assistant to the surgeon (me), anaesthetist (Carlos), instrument or scrub nurse (me), and circulating nurse (Mayra) who is the link between the operating table and the rest of the equipment and instruments in the theatre.

blood vessels with mosquito forceps, with my naked hands dyed with Merthiolate, the characteristic whistling thrum of an incoming mortar round petrified us.

'Get down!' I shouted, 'and don't get contaminated, we're out of gloves!'

The shell landed in the coffee fields above the hacienda about 100 metres away. Virtually as one, we stood up again and continued operating. René was about to open the uterus when we heard a new round approaching. This time there was no need to warn anyone. We all hit the ground face down, with our hands in the air leaning on our elbows. This time, the shell landed no more than 50 metres from us and we could feel the impact.

Again, we stood up quickly and got back to work. With admirable calm and great agility, René opened the uterus and delivered the baby.

The umbilical cord was disproportionately long and was wrapped around the baby's neck twice. This was the reason why the foetus didn't engage and the reason for the foetal distress. René skilfully freed the neck from the cord, while I clamped it. Then I cut it and rushed the infant, who looked somewhat bruised and flaccid, to the stand where the DeLee suction catheter[19] was. I pulled down my mask, took the suction catheter between my lips and suctioned all the secretions from the baby's mouth and nose. This stimulated him and he reacted. As he took his first breath and let out a cry, I sighed in relief.

19 DeLee suction catheter: A device with an air trap and a reservoir located between the resuscitator and the newborn that is used to suction the secretions that obstruct the airway, helping the baby to take its first breath.

'It's a boy!' I said to Rebequita, and that's when I noticed her face contorting with terror. A new mortar shell was approaching, which I only noticed just then and it sounded like it was going to fall very close by.

'Cover him, Felipe!' Rebequita screamed at me with emotive maternal instinct.

I barely managed to wrap up the baby and once again we threw ourselves to the ground. They must have an observer who is correcting the aim,[20] I said to myself, because each time they're hitting closer. The explosion was terrible and we felt the expansion wave. The shell had fallen on a house three doors down, on what had been the pharmacy. When we got up, I saw that René had taken the precaution to cover Rebequita's open abdomen before hitting the floor. Two pieces of roof tile were on the canvas that was serving as the operative field. With impressive speed (he had already delivered the placenta and injected oxytocin in the uterine muscle), René sutured the uterus and abdominal wall. He finished sewing her up right when we heard a new projectile approach. It landed in the yard of a house two doors down from where we were, near the front door. In the midst of a cloud of dust, smoke and the acrid odour of gunpowder, René and I put Rebequita and the baby on a stretcher, picked up our rucksacks (which were always ready for a sudden retreat) and grabbed the stretcher. René took the head and I took the foot, while Carlos held up the IV and ran next to us. Mayra, who had also helped us during the operation, followed a little behind, carrying the surgical instruments we had used.

Now, no one was left in the hospital. Everyone had gotten out and Eliseo, who was up ahead by himself crouching among some rocks, signalled for us to join him. As soon as we reached Eliseo, two more shells directly hit the house, precisely on our beloved and improvised operating theatre.

[20] Firing a mortar requires a gunner to handle the weapon and ideally an observer with long-range binoculars who observes, gives the gunner coordinates and corrects the aim.

'Those would have blown us to smithereens,' Carlos said calmly. 'Now, let's pick up the pace to catch up with the column.'

Guinda

When we got to Palmo Chacho, our next stop, we met up with all the *sanitarios* and the non-ambulatory patients.

There were 14 patients in all (we had evacuated those with minor wounds and seven hammock-bound patients only three days earlier) and there were 28 of us; that is, exactly two per patient, the minimum number required. (In normal conditions, we would assign up to six carriers per patient, so they could take turns during the journey.)

However, we couldn't travel without front and rear guards. It would have been insane, especially knowing that we would have to hike toward the northwest for a good distance before changing direction; that is, toward the position abandoned by the FAL, where at any moment we might run into enemy troops. In addition, it was evident from the mortar fire that the hospital had been located and that they must have had it under observation, since they had been correcting their aim. This meant that they could have located our retreat route to pursue us, which is why we needed someone to cover the retreat. This, in turn, meant that we could only carry 13 patients and that we would have to abandon one of them. When I realized this, my heart clenched and I called to René.

'Who's the most critical patient?' I asked, without letting him know what I was thinking.

'Donaldo,' he said. 'He's been in a coma since the operation. Yesterday he developed sepsis and today's he's got kidney failure. I doubt he'll make it through the night.'

A week earlier we had operated on Donaldo. He was just 17 years old and had come in with a bullet wound in the upper right quadrant of his abdomen, with a horrible exit wound in the lumbar region. The operation was extremely bloody. His liver was

severed in two and his abdominal cavity was filled with blood. It was almost impossible to stanch the bleeding and we used up our entire reserve of Gelfoam (a kind of biodegradable gauze) to plug the liver. He finally stopped bleeding, though I don't know if it was from shock or the Gelfoam, and we were able to examine the other organs. He had four intestinal perforations and the right kidney was 75 per cent destroyed, so we had to remove it. Despite René's skill, the operation lasted almost six hours and when we finished, his blood pressure was zero.

'Lay him down with the stretcher about a hundred yards into the coffee grove, and leave him with a slow drip with the antibiotic in his IV. We can't take him. We'll need one man as front guard and another as rear guard for the security of the column and that means two hammock-bearers less.'

'But . . .'

'No buts. This is an order and this is not the time to argue about it. I assume responsibility. Send me Eliseo. He'll be the front guard.'

We only had two weapons: an old M-1 carbine, a survivor of

the Second World War, with 50 rounds, and my revolver with six bullets in the chamber and 18 in reserve.

I instructed Eliseo to advance 50 metres in front of the column and carefully explore as he moved forward. If he saw the enemy, he must be the first to fire and ensure at least one casualty[21] and that way we'd have the advantage of surprise. He should retreat toward the south, shooting to attract enemy fire, while we, with the patients, would move silently northward and we'd meet up in Los Alpes, the second stop on the retreat route.

I would cover the rear with my revolver in the same way to facilitate the evacuation of the patients if it turned out the army was pursuing us. In my absence, Carlos Barbón would be in command of the column.

As soon as they had hidden Donaldo I gave the order to commence the march and to remain completely silent throughout the trip. I remained behind waiting for the column to get ahead a bit so that I wasn't too close to them. When I calculated that there was a prudent distance between us, I began my hike bringing up the rear.

A few minutes later, the last pair of stretcher-bearers came back and whispered to me, 'An enemy column is coming about 50 metres above us. Luckily, we saw them first.'

'And the others?'

'They're already ahead. I don't think they detected us. We lagged behind because the patient's IV had come out and we were searching for a vein when we sensed their presence. They'll pass by here any minute now.'

'Okay,' I said. 'The only thing we can do is take cover. Hide yourselves well. If they see me, I'll open fire and you'll retreat to the west and I'll fire southward, as we'd agreed.'

We covered ourselves with branches and began the wait. Fifteen minutes later we saw them through the foliage. They were

[21] A guerrilla tactic to have an immediate impact on enemy troop morale, slow them down and use up their resources.

wearing a camouflage uniform I was seeing for the first time and they were moving slowly towards the Barrios plantation. They had a mine detector at the front and were walking in two parallel columns. No doubt because of the fear of land mines, neither column was walking on the path, but rather in the coffee grove. I readied my revolver and braced it against a rock to steady my aim. I didn't want to miss on the first shot, which could make the difference. However, they didn't detect us. There were about 60 of them and they passed by around 20 metres from where we were.

Shortly after, we caught up with the rest of the column and together arrived at Los Alpes around four in the afternoon. Our hands were raw and we were all exhausted from carrying with no relief. We expected the *masas* – civilian supporters – to be there to supposedly help us carry the patients, but the mortar fire over Barrios had frightened them and they'd left, leaving behind them a broad swath heading toward the summit of the volcano. Just then, we started at a heavy fusillade less than 500 metres away in the direction of Barrios.

'They must have run into the *compas*,' Eliseo told me.

'Anything could happen. We need to prepare,' I told him. 'We have to hide the wounded in the bush, because the people can't carry any more and won't be able to run with them if they catch up with us. Put a lookout in the direction where we heard the fighting while we hide the wounded.'

About 15 minutes later, Eliseo returned, accompanied by Juanón, the commander of the Frente, and his entire military staff.

Juanón turned to me and said, 'What are you still doing here, Felipe?'

'The *masas* didn't wait for us and we can't carry the patients alone. The column is advancing very slowly. What was that shooting about?'

'It was with us. Two of my *compas* got lost, but I don't think they're wounded, because they were seen retreating in another direction. They'll show up soon. But you can't stay here. The enemy

is definitely going to show up soon and our technical personnel are very valuable and we will continue to need them. You need to see it this way. There's no way to replace the staff of the Hospital del Frente.'

'Look,' I said, 'we can't abandon the wounded. Let's do something: help us hide them and half of the staff will stay with them. The other half of the staff can go with you and you can send people to pick us up later tonight after the danger has passed. In any case, if the enemy comes here, they'll most likely follow the trail left by the *masas* and won't even notice us.'

'All right,' Juanón said, 'I'll also leave you three rifles just in case. I'll send for you at 8:00 PM'

When we'd finished hiding the patients, I called Carlos over and said: 'Carlos, I don't think we need to risk half of the staff in this. In any case, Juanón will send bearers tonight. I'll stay here with Mayra, Toño, Eliseo and Tomás. All the rest of you go with Juanón. Tell René and the others so that they leave as soon as possible.'

After the *compas* left, I set out to check on the camouflage for the stretchers and to set up the line of fire with the three rifles, my revolver and the carbine. That's when I noticed René, who had stayed behind, even though he could have left for safety.

It was an act of quiet heroism and tremendous sensitivity and it deeply moved me. However, I was also very annoyed. If René fell, the loss would be irreparable.

'I'm grateful for your solidarity,' I told him with emotion in my voice, 'but it was a reckless thing to do. In the future, you should also think about those who have yet to be wounded in this war and will need your services.'

I continued organizing the armed *compas* and finally I stretched out next to Eliseo.

'Eliseo, if there's fighting, don't use up all the bullets. Save the last one for yourself. In any case, I don't want to end up in their hands alive. I was already a prisoner once and I don't want to be tortured again.'

'Felipe, Felipe,' a voice whispered behind me.

I turned around and saw that it was 'Trinchera', named after the trenches he fought in. He was one of the wounded, an 18-year-old combatant who had been shot in the femur almost a year ago. After curing him of the chronic osteomyelitis that had kept him laid up for over seven months, his youthful carelessness and the flirtatious attention of one of the *sanitarias* caused the recently-formed bone callus to re-fracture and his hospital stay to be prolonged. He was the most veteran patient and his chronic illness had made him part of the everyday landscape of the Hospital del Frente. Normally, he was contagiously optimistic and endeared himself to everyone.

'Save a bullet for me, too, please,' he told me, in the most natural way possible and with his usual smile.

Around 5:30 in the evening, an enemy column arrived. They came to about ten metres away from the underbrush where we were crouched. We could hear them clearly and could even see the laces on their military boots. Those of us who were armed were lying down and aiming towards the soldiers. We held our breath and listened until we could even hear our own heartbeats. They stopped, and seeing the swath left by the *masas*, set off to follow it. But shortly after they returned and left in the direction of Barrios.

At 8:00 PM, the *compas* that Juanón promised arrived and we began the march to El Carmen farm. El Carmen was behind enemy lines and if we managed to get there without mishap we'd be outside the area of the military operation and in relative safety. The trip was hard. The paths were overgrown and disappeared in some spots because they hadn't been used for a long time and the patients made the march even more difficult. At four in the morning we arrived at El Carmen. There we found around 60 guerrilla fighters and the Frente's military staff. A tremendous sensation of relief invaded us. We put the stretchers with the wounded on the ground and we immediately fell asleep at their side. This time we were safe!

However, the pleasure didn't last long. Fifteen minutes later I felt someone shaking me roughly. I forced my eyes open, with the urge to curse out the inopportune and inconsiderate jerk who was daring to interrupt my richly deserved rest, when I realized it was Luisón. Half awake, I listened to what he had to say.

'You can't stay here Felipe,' he explained. 'The Tracking Unit (which listened in on intercepted enemy radio conversations) says that the enemy detected some of our movements in this zone and they will probably explore tomorrow. We're preparing a good reception for them, but we need to be very mobile and use all available combatants, so we won't be able to guard you and it would be better for you to leave the zone. You should head down toward Tepetitán.'

Hearing this, I jerked awake and began waking up everyone to continue the march.

'Get up! Get up everyone! We still have a ways to go. Hurry up! Wake up! We have to get there before dawn.'

Everyone was griping since almost all of us were on the verge of collapse. I was not used to carrying patients and my hands were blistered from the wooden stretcher bars and both my shoulders were bruised and aching from the bamboo poles used to carry the hammocks.

'Let's go!' I said. 'The enemy is going to attack at daylight. Hurry up! The route is all downhill and in an hour we'll be out of danger.'

Grudgingly, we started the march again. We were almost trotting to get to our destination as quickly as possible. Forty-five minutes later it was almost full daylight. I was ahead of the column and when I turned around to look behind me my hair stood on end. The route we had just taken was almost completely bare of vegetation and the column was extremely long. If we kept up at the same rate, the enemy would spot us in short order because the reconnaissance planes had already begun their monotonous buzzing in search of guerrilla columns.

'Eliseo, I think we've walked enough. Let's get off the path and find a place to spend the day.'

Soon we were in a small copse. It was almost six in the morning. We lowered the patients and fell exhausted by their sides. I didn't remember to organize the sentries and no one reminded me, that's how tired I was. When I awoke, the sun was full on my face. It was one in the afternoon and I was on rocky ground. I had no idea how I'd been able to sleep there, without even taking off my rucksack. Old Man Simón was across from me, eating a papaya along with honey. His good-natured, open smile filled me with peace of mind.

'Want some, Felipe?' he asked, handing me an enormous slice of fruit and a piece of honeycomb dripping with honey.

I didn't answer, and instead, pounced on the papaya and honey, since by then we had gone almost three days without eating and walking day and night. Simón sliced up two more papayas and while he gave me more honey and observed me contentedly with his scraggly-toothed smile, worn by the years and the war, he explained that about a hundred metres away he'd found a papaya grove and some fifty bee hives. He'd only opened one hive to 'milk' it, since he knew a lot about beekeeping and knew how to do so without damaging the frames, the bees or the structure of the hive.

'I have to organize the sentries,' I said as I stood up. 'If not, they're going to catch us like little lambs.'

'Don't worry. Barbón already organized them. It's not your turn until five in the afternoon. Also, René already did rounds and gave instructions. Keep on sleeping. I'll get you if any communication comes in from Juanón. In any case, we have nothing to do but wait.'

The *guinda*, as we called these tactical retreats during invasions by the government army, would last two more weeks, every one of its days as dramatic as those told here. By the time it ended, with the exception of Donaldo, the patient left in Palmo Chacho, and a civilian teenager whose arm we'd recently amputated and who died crossing the Lempa River, we didn't lose any more patients or a single member of our extremely valuable and experienced crew.

Every one of them went far beyond the Hippocratic Oath, which pales in comparison to the magnitude of the sacrifice and solidarity they freely bestowed during that intense and unrepeatable experience and their exceptional bequest of humanity.

Old Man Simón's Miraculous Still

During the months following the General Offensive of 1981, the rebel-held areas went through very difficult times. Our forces had depleted almost all their arsenals and militarily the offensive had not obtained the expected results. As a consequence, we were forced to retreat, and the army, which fortunately was not very capable either, nor had very high morale, mounted operations to tighten the noose around our zones with the idea of choking us off.

Given their fear of raiding our territories because of the constant casualties they would suffer during those operations, the army focused its strategy on terrorizing the civilian population with these noose operations, to split us off from them.

Any civilian moving about the periphery of our controlled zones would be captured, interrogated, and meticulously searched for weapons, compromising literature, and, naturally, medical supplies. If they were caught with more than ten aspirin or any other medicine in unusual quantities, they could be tortured and mercilessly murdered. In fact, the army would also disappear or kill civilians without any motive as part of this terror strategy. This severely reduced our supplies, which we would have to bring in. It became especially difficult to get intravenous solutions. Little by little, we used up our reserves and that's when we decided to take on the task of making our own solutions.

René (Eduardo Coto), Federico (the Dutch physician) and I met to figure out a way to do it. We started by reminding ourselves that physiological solution[22] is a normal saline solution, which can be prepared if you have distilled water (without impurities), sodium chloride (salt), and bicarbonate of soda (baking soda).

The challenge was not easy: In very general terms, we would have to find a way to combine 1 litre of distilled water with 5 grams of salt and 2.5 grams of bicarbonate, to obtain 1 litre of normal saline solution. All this had to be done under sterile conditions, with no impurities and with a high degree of precision in the

[22] Fluid with an electrolyte composition similar to bodily fluids, which can be used to replace blood volume following a sudden and substantial loss of fluids such as with intense diarrhoea or haemorrhaging, to prevent or reverse shock (collapse of the cardiovascular system) and ensuing death.

measurements and in addition, with the resources that we had in the zone, with the idea of having sustained production with satisfactory quality and quantity.

As we began, we sent an SOS to our collaborators in San Salvador asking them get us chemically pure sodium chloride and bicarbonate, as we couldn't run the risk of introducing foreign bodies into our patients.

Then we turned our efforts to figuring out how to make distilled water.

At first, we thought of collecting rainwater. But we soon realized how sickening this idea was when we saw the turbidity of this water. So, we began boiling water and trying to capture the condensed vapour in other containers.

The solution came from Simón, an old *campesino*, who was in charge of obtaining supplies for the hospital. After seeing our multiple attempts to build a condenser for the vapour from the water we were boiling fail again and again, he said: 'Listen, *Compa*, that thing looks like a still like the one my father used to make moonshine. Why don't we try making one of those?'

René and Federico hit the ground running and a month later, after successive attempts that we improved as we went along, we had built a rustic still out of a milking can, where we put the water to distil, which we boiled over a wood fire at its base. On top of this first container, we had designed, built and welded a cone-shaped cap, connected at the top to a downward-sloping tube. At the other end of the tube, we had adapted another identical container where we collected the condensed water, which was now distilled water. Later, we hooked up two of the devices in sequence, from which we obtained double-distilled water, which was totally clear, and according to the tests done by our collaborators in San Salvador, free of any type of impurities.

In the meantime, we had received our first delivery of two pounds of chemically pure sodium chloride and one pound of bicarbonate, enough to make close to 200 litres of IV solution, which would strategically solve the problem, if and when we actually made it.

Next, we had to figure out how to weigh exactly 5 grams of sodium chloride and 2.5 grams of bicarbonate, which would then be mixed with the double-distilled water. Help came from our basic knowledge of pure sciences that we studied during our time taking the core curriculum at the national university. I remembered that the weight of a cubic centimetre of distilled water was exactly one gram. Since we had ampoules of distilled water in different amounts (2 cc, 5 cc) to use as weights, we'd have no problem making combinations such as adding five grams of bicarbonate to two litres of water and five grams of sodium chloride to one litre. The serious problem was how to accurately weigh the salt and the bicarbonate.

This time, it was the physics we'd learned in the core curriculum that came to our aid. I remembered the Law of the Lever that applied to the balance-beam scale: the product of the effort by its arm equals the product of the resistance by its arm. Soon we set out to build a scale, again with Simón's help. We would place the ampoules of distilled water with known quantities on one pan and on the other pan the salt or bicarbonate that we needed, until the scales balanced.

The first scales were very unstable and did not detect significant variations of salt, bicarbonate or both due to the instability of the needle. So, to increase the scales' sensitivity,[23] we made them with enormous arms of bamboo. These were so sensitive, that the slightest current of air made them fluctuate, until we made a sort of plastic tent that protected them from the breeze. This way, we solved the problem of sensitivity and accuracy in the measurement.

Finally, to prevent bacteria from contaminating the prepared solution during handling when it was bottled and sealed, we reboiled the sealed bottles in an adobe bread oven, the kind which is

[23] According the Law of the Lever, as the arm gets longer, small changes in the effort or the resistance become much more perceptible; i.e. the scales become more sensitive.

common in rural areas.

To ensure its safety, we conducted several trials with experimental animals, primarily dogs. We monitored their vital signs as we gave them transfusions of the solution. Simón watched us amazed and annoyed that after so much effort had gone into producing the famous solutions, they would end up being given to stray dogs. We gave the dogs transfusions over and over without detecting any negative reactions. Even so, we still didn't dare use the solution with our *compañeros*.

One day of many, a call came over the two-way radio we had in the hospital alerting us that we had a casualty in a skirmish with National Guardsmen on the Tecoluca–San Vicente road and that they'd be arriving with him in a few minutes. They'd given him first aid but even so, he'd lost a lot of blood. We readied our surgical materials and personnel and about half an hour later we received the patient. He had been shot by a 7.62 mm cartridge from a G3 rifle above his right knee, which had fractured the femur and severed the femoral artery and we would have no choice but to amputate his leg. The unit's *sanitario* had managed to control the haemorrhaging in the line of fire with a tourniquet, but the patient had lost a copious amount of blood and arrived in shock. His heart was racing, his blood pressure had plummeted and he was white as a sheet. To top it off, his blood type was B positive, which is very rare, and we didn't have any compatible donors.

'Okay,' René said, 'this is it. Either we give him our homemade solution or he's going to die on us.'

'Mayra,' he said to a *sanitaria*, 'start a wide-open IV in each arm.'

Mayra nimbly accessed the combatant's collapsed veins and soon he began to respond and to come out of shock. We needed to give him four litres immediately, which improved him enough to be able to amputate his leg relatively safely. In all, we ended up giving him around ten litres of homemade IV solution. His recovery was quite quick and he had no complications, and no reaction at all to the solution we gave him.

Federico and Simón were beside themselves with joy. René and I were just as happy, and that night we paid ourselves back with a long night-time chat with a double ration of coffee, which we accompanied with sweet rolls, an exceptional treat in our controlled territory, a find from Simón's rummaging around. We had solved the problem of the IVs with minimal resources and a little bit of ingenuity.

From then on, we never had to buy IV solution or put our collaborators' lives in jeopardy by trying to smuggle it into the rebel-held area. When we told the other battle fronts of our success, we were deluged with requests to accept people and train them in the production of homemade IV solution, which we did eagerly, appointing Simón instructor-in-chief. He did an exquisite job, teaching the others how to make stills and how to carry out the process from start to finish.

A Cool Explosive

Preserving medicines that required refrigeration was a constant headache. We had no electricity, ice chests only kept them cold for a few hours, and forget about getting generators for electricity and cooling in the highly mobile conditions of war. We had thought up many alternatives, from taking the medicines to the top of the volcano where temperatures were cool and steady, to storing them in the periphery of the controlled territory in the homes of collaborators in the expansion zones.[24] Both strategies worked, but it was extremely difficult to gather medicines in sufficient quantities when we needed them.

Blood typing of combatants was also a strategic issue, since it helped us to know their blood type if they got wounded, and to rapidly locate potential donors.

The command of the Paracentral Front had delegated to me the relationship with the International Committee of the Red Cross (ICRC) to review issues such as respect for human rights, handing over soldiers and officers captured as prisoners of war, and the evacuation of disabled combatants. During this contact, which I had with some regularity, the ICRC would occasionally give us blood collection bags and typing sera, but these needed refrigeration or they would rapidly lose their effectiveness.

Several times we resorted to assembling our military units in the vicinity of our interviews with the ICRC, for the purpose of typing our combatants as soon as we finished the meeting. However, the army eventually detected this manoeuvre and we had to give it up, making the refrigeration problem increasingly dire and its resolution urgent.

One day, when I went to conduct a health inspection at the explosives workshop in the zone, I got there when they were making ammonium nitrate, which was used as the most voluminous component (85 per cent) of the explosive mixture for homemade guerrilla grenades and land mines, as well as for anti-armoured vehicle devices.

The ammonium nitrate was being manufactured in response to increased government control over the product, which was used as fertilizer in the coffee fields. To satisfy my curiosity, they explained that it was made by mixing nitric acid with ammonia, which a network of collaborators would smuggle into the front in

[24] Expansion: Undefined territory located on the periphery of the guerrilla-controlled zones. A sort of no-man's land, it was the scene of frequent battles where enemy units and our units moved with the same insecurity.

liquid form in enormous barrels.

The mixture was made in large porcelain bowls out-of-doors because it gave off vapour and, this is what caught my eye, a large amount of heat, which is why the process had to be done slowly to prevent dangerous accidents.

If the reaction is exothermic, I thought, then the product must be endothermic.

'Rebequita, and the nitrate that you make, is it cool?' I asked our clever artisanal chemist.

'Frigid, *Compa*!' she answered. 'Come see for yourself.'

The nitrate was also chemically pure, as opposed to the fertilizer that was sold for farming, which was usually contaminated. It was a very fine white powder and it was cool in temperature. I asked her to give me about five pounds and went to see Simón.

'Simón, I need some containers we can line with this nitrate.'

In a few days, Simón had figured it out, making double-sided boxes out of Styrofoam where we could keep the medicines that needed to be refrigerated, which would be surrounded by nitrate. The idea to use Styrofoam was great because it strengthened the endothermic reaction and lowered the temperature even more. Soon we were storing antibiotics and our precious blood typing sera in these coolers. Our collaborators in the expansion zone breathed a sigh of relief when they learned that they would no longer have to store compromising medicines in their refrigerators. Our couriers were also relieved, when they found out that their long night-time hikes to collect medicines by going from house to house would no longer be necessary.

Scabies

Scabies, caused by a mite that is a minute parasite of the skin, gave us serious problems. We would frequently inspect the camps and we would train combatants as *sanitarios*, and even though we emphasized hygiene and daily bathing, this was not always possible and the camps could be easy prey to an epidemic if a combatant caught the bug. The itching was unbearable and people with scabies would often get secondary infections from scratching, especially if their nails were not very clean.

Federico, the Dutch doctor, was the first to notice that, at least on the San Vicente volcano, almost all the combatants used the same type of soap, which was homemade from the fruit of the *aceituno*[25] tree (they called it '*jucumico*' soap, though no one could tell me the origin or meaning of this name). Federico used this soap himself, which was also good for dandruff, and he soon noticed that there were only a few people who made it, almost all of them elderly *campesinas* in the civilian population who were living in the controlled zone and who earned a few extra cents from this product of their labour.

From his observation, he rapidly came up with the suggestion that it would help to add an ingredient to prevent scabies when the soap was being made. We soon learned from some dermatologist friends that the best thing we could do would be to add sulphur to

[25] *Simarouba glauca* is a tree native to Central America that resembles the olive trees of Spain, and was thus given the name *aceituno*, which means olive in Spanish. *Jucumico* is probably derived from an indigenous name for the tree.—*Tr.*

the soap. Just like with the salt for the IV solutions, we soon figured out how to obtain 'dusting sulphur', which is sulphur powder, and we started giving it to the ladies so they could add it to the soap recipe. In turn, we promised that we would recommend that the combatants buy their soap at the houses where sulphur was added.

We never had problems with epidemic scabies again.

The Battle Against Pain

Another problem we faced with growing distress was the shortage of potent analgesics. In addition to the cordon and search tactics that the army used on the civilian population in the periphery around our controlled zones, drugs such as morphine and others like it are controlled substances due to their enormous potential to cause addiction. No wonder morphine derives its name from Morpheus, the Greek god of dreams.

We guarded our few ampoules of morphine like treasure, only using them in truly drastic cases when the patient's pain was unbearable. Our supplies in these cases came from the health sector – almost always from nurses and doctors who had access to these controlled drugs.

The doctors would usually resort to the device of prescribing them to imaginary patients. Nurses, in turn, would report that they had broken an ampoule while transporting it. Their supervisors would demand to see the label and the glass fragments of the 'broken' ampoule, so before reporting the loss, they would carefully remove the label and break another ampoule of a similar size and colour to present as proof. All of this required great courage and conviction in what they were doing, and therefore it wasn't that frequent. Moreover, due to the controls, doctors could not indefinitely prescribe these drugs to their imaginary patients without raising suspicions.

As a result, potent analgesics came to us on the war front in dribs and drabs.

On one occasion in late 1982, Douglas Santamaría,[26] who had recently assumed the position of military commander of the Paracentral Front, came to the hospital to talk to me.

'Hey, Felipe, I brought you this thing that a collaborator passed on to me. He says it's good for pain, that some gringo sympathisers sent it. See if it's good for anything.'

'Thanks, Douglas,' I said, 'but didn't he tell you anything else? It's name? Where it's from? It's active ingredient? Anything that could give us an inkling? It's kind of difficult to know what the hell this is, much less give it to someone without having more information.'

'Nothing else. I'm passing it on to you just like they gave it to me. Try to see if someone in Metro[27] can figure it out. Maybe some lab tech.'

'Okay. We'll see what we can do.'

It was a small bottle labelled as a vitamin supplement for babies and it contained about 20 grams of a very fine white powder, similar to baking soda. About three weeks later, I had to go into San Salvador to buy some medicines that had run out. I remembered the little bottle with the white powder and threw it in my bag to see if I could do something with it.

Leaving the controlled zones to travel to Metro was not without danger. We had to travel by bus from the periphery of the zone, trying not to arouse suspicion, especially during that vulnerable moment when boarding the bus. Usually, we'd leave our camp on the volcano at sundown on the night before, so we could cross the Zacatecoluca–San Vicente road at night, to keep the army from detecting us. Then we'd get to the zone known as Las Pampas, where we'd rest for a few minutes before setting off again, walking in

[26] Eduardo Linares, a member of San Salvador's City Council when the first edition of this book came out, was one of the most brilliant, ingenious, and charismatic military commanders of the Popular Forces of Liberation (FPL). He forged the Vanguard Units and was a very important player in most of the FPL's strategic military strikes during the war.

[27] Metropolitan San Salvador.

absolute silence under cover of the shadows, for about four hours, until arriving at the home of a collaborator or sympathiser in the expansion zone located near the coastal highway, fairly far from the periphery of the controlled zone. There, we'd rest for a couple of hours until dawn and then we'd go through a metamorphosis. We'd put down our weapons, take off our military uniforms, shave our long beards and dress like any local from the area. Then, we'd walk to the highway, wait for the bus and set off to San Salvador, where we'd usually arrive around mid-day.

When arriving in Metro, we'd routinely contact Mextli,[28] who was in charge of logistical supplies that would be gathered with help from collaborators and international solidarity groups, which she would send to our zones. Mextli would find us a place to stay in the home of a collaborator for the two to three days we'd spend in San Salvador.

On that occasion, after having purchased gauze, antiseptic soap, antibiotics and other medicines we were low on, I remembered the little bottle and decided to find out what it was. I found a public telephone and called Urí Cardoza,[29] an old co-worker in the Department of Physiology and Pharmacology of the Medical School at the University of El Salvador.

'Hi, Urí! I'm in San Salvador. You know who this is, right?'

'Guayo! I'm so happy to hear from you! What have you been up to? They're going to kill you! And on the way they're going to take me with you. What are doing here?'

'I need to see you so you can help me with something. Don't worry, it's not dangerous. Do you have some time right now? I want to give you something and I can deliver it personally or send it with someone else who's completely trustworthy.'

[28] Nelly Cacao, a Salvadoran physician who was later captured by the death squads, who tortured her horribly before killing her. Nelly knew a lot of valuable information and many collaborators and supply routes to the war fronts, but the death squads did not manage to get any information from her.

[29] Urí Cardoza Soto, at that time an instructor at the University of El Salvador.

Several hours later, a relative of mine delivered a note and the bottle with the mysterious white powder to her, asking her to test it to figure out what it was and telling her that we suspected that it could be morphine or heroin.

'Don't worry, Guayo, I'll talk to Noemí,[30] she works in Carlos Vargas'[31] lab. I'm sure he'll lend us his lab. How will I get word to you?'

'Don't worry. I'll find you.'

Once Urí contacted Noemí, she in turn got in touch with Carlos and the two of them mobilized an entire team of experts who were sympathetic to the cause, to get the reagents and the stabilizers, to conduct the dilutions, and to do the laboratory tests, which even included tests on lab animals to test the effectiveness of the drug on elevating the pain threshold. As a result, two weeks later we had our answer: extremely pure morphine. And, a month later, we had in our hands, sent by Urí, 40 five-cc injectable vials, each containing 10 mg of morphine per cc.

The news was so good we couldn't believe it. The analgesic dose for morphine is 10 milligrams and we would now have enough doses for several years of war.

When we would administer morphine to a combatant, it would not only suppress their pain, but also cause the well-known euphoric effect responsible for eventual addiction to the drug. So, to play it safe and to keep the combatants from knowing what it was, René baptised it '*aguantacaína*' (something like 'endurocaine'), a name that did not allude at all to Morpheus, nor did it reflect the enormous collective effort that had been put into play to obtain it.

[30] Noemí Gómez, instructor at the University of El Salvador.

[31] Physician, professor in the Department of Physiology and Pharmacology of the Medical School of the University of El Salvador. He was captured by government forces when leaving his private clinic in 1982 and never seen again.

FRUSTRATED CONVERSATION WITH FERNANDO OÑA

Date: Mon, 29 Jan 2007 01:50:03 -0600 (CST)
From: porsiviajo <porsiviajo@xxx.xxx>
Subject: Frustrated Conversation
To: periodicopcion@xxx.xxx

Greetings Fernando,[1]

I was so happy to see you, and I was also very sorry that we didn't get to talk more in depth. The suspension of activities due to the death of the Minister of Defence of Ecuador and another bunch of things and tasks kept us from getting in touch again. We certainly would have found many topics of common interest, but it wasn't possible to share anything, much less learn what your main interest was at the time. In any case, I want to share an anecdote about something that happened recently that brought back memories from a long time ago.

Recently, an old comrade in arms in the guerrilla army sent me some writings that I had given up for lost. They were old poems written in the heat of war, in the mountains, between one battle and the next. I still don't know how they ended up in his hands or where he found them.

They came at an opportune moment. It turns out that a couple of days ago, an uncle on my father's side of the family, who is very given to the arts, sent me a CD of a child choir organized by him in the remote Honduran town where he lives. In the note that accompanied the CD he expressed his apprehension that the

[1] Fernando Oña, journalist, editor of the Ecuadoran newspaper *Opción*.

content of the disc would probably not be to my liking.

To better understand how I responded to him, I want to give you a little background of the special relationship we had.

When I was very young, we used to spend the vacation at the end of the school year at my grandfather's house, in the same town where this uncle lives. This town was something like García Márquez's Macondo. No motor vehicle had ever entered the town and the only contact with the outside world was a two-engine airplane that would arrive once a week. This was quite the event and was watched by the entire little community, which would turn out on the dirt and grass landing strip to see who was arriving and who was leaving town.

So, our two months of vacation went by there with our paternal grandparents and another 15 cousins around our age, and we did nothing but make mischief, or ride horses with our grandfather to check on the coffee plantation or help him herd his cattle into different pastures. This is how we spent our bucolic existence trying to forget that school was going to start again soon. As expected, our Macondo did not have electricity (even though this was in the early 1960s) and so the village literally went into suspended animation around 6:30 in the evening at sundown.

With my citified, more cosmopolitan customs of the time, this forced suspension of activities was the only blemish on that paradisiacal place. It didn't take me long to find the answer to my nocturnal restlessness in Uncle Quique,[2] the uncle of yore. He was an amazing character who would listen to long-play records by classical musicians on a wind-up gramophone, who painted oil portraits and landscapes, who would organize the children in parish choirs, and who had rare books and always something interesting to talk about in that forgotten corner of the world.

After the end of our day's youthful adventures, I would be on the lookout for any adult who would be going to visit Uncle

[2] Enrique Rodezno, a native and resident of the town of San Marcos Ocotepeque, Honduras.

Quique to go along with them, because we'd have to walk several blocks in the pitch dark and I wasn't allowed to go alone. He would always welcome us and would give us some delicious morsel and something to drink, occasionally wine, the story of which he would tell us at length while I learned to savour it. His living room, decorated in a refined manner with his oil paintings and souvenirs from other lands, was lit with the soft light of kerosene lanterns that created a magical, welcoming and stimulating environment.

I think he was also very intrigued by this lad who had not yet reached adolescence and who was interested in his paintings and books and questioned his opinions and judgements.

My coming of age abruptly interrupted this relationship and my demanding medical school studies, the war between El Salvador and Honduras in 1969 and the civil war in El Salvador kept us apart for almost 30 years. I saw Uncle Quique briefly following the signing of the Peace Accords in El Salvador, during a short visit to Honduras with some friends. The town had grown – many streets, many vehicles, electricity, Internet, pubs, brothels, pool halls, etc. Uncle Quique's house across from the town square had been replaced by a modern supermarket and the garden that had adorned the entrance to the house was also gone. I asked for his address and was sent to the outskirts of town by the nearby hills. I went there and found him painting. He had sold his old home when he could no longer stand the noise and the advent of modern life. He was still surrounded by the same magical ambience that fascinated me during my youth. Unfortunately, my friends were in a hurry and I only had time to greet him quickly and express my joy at finding him healthy and active.

A couple of years ago I saw him again very briefly and he asked for my address. I hadn't heard from him until I received the CD I mentioned at the beginning of this e-mail and the note in which he expressed his fears that my character and romanticism had probably hardened because of the war and my revolutionary concerns.

I'm attaching the note I sent to answer him, which includes

the old guerrilla poems. I don't expect you to like them – they don't have much literary value – but they reflect a little bit of the intensity of those times during the struggle, which I remember caught your attention when you interviewed me in *Opción* during the preparatory meeting for the Second People's Health Assembly, when we returned from Ingapirca.[3]

Fraternally and fondly,

Eduardo

Letter to Uncle Quique

Dear Uncle Quique,

I must confess that your note sent me diving into deep musings about your judgement on my probable loss of romanticism and sensitivity because of the civil war.

Would Uncle Quique think, I asked myself, that I am really unfeeling, tough and repressive? I wonder if he thinks that the war covered me in armour, a mixture of savagery and stoicism that keep me from expressing any love or tenderness at all. Or perhaps, despite his beloved culture, could Uncle Quique have fallen victim to the stereotypical image that people try to create of revolutionaries as cruel and ruthless?

Well, I should say in my defence that I am like any flesh and blood mortal, sensitive to the love and affection of my fellow humans, perhaps (and this in my capacity as a revolutionary) more sensitive and with thinner skin than they have to these and other sublime feelings. Those of us who rose up in arms did not do so for love of war or a desire to make our neighbours suffer or from petty aspirations of power. We were moved by a deep feeling of love for humanity.

Our indignation in the face of injustice came from a

[3] An Inca fort in the Ecuadorean province of Cañar, it is a pre-Colombian jewel that means 'Inca Wall', temple of the gods, and was built in the 15th century by the Inca Huayna Cápac to worship the sun god, on top of the ruins of the Cañari Indians who had lived there.

consequence of that love: from a conscious intolerance to pain, to poverty and to inequality, especially if the latter are unjust, unnecessary and preventable.[4] I don't believe that the poor are that way because of divine command. Therefore, I cannot resign myself to accept it as something that should be part of our normal landscape. Neither do I blame the poor for their poverty. Thus, I cannot reproach them for the illnesses of their children or for the ignorance that has been imposed on them through unchecked exploitation or the deliberate suppression of opportunities. It fills me with indignation that poverty coexists with wastefulness and luxury, which because of its excesses is insulting, lacerating and deplorable. I believe (and it is scientifically demonstrable) that poverty is a social product constructed and perpetuated by an unjust society.

Certainly the war was incredibly hard, demanding, all consuming. During the war I experienced moments of intense joy, such as when I saw beloved *compañeros* return uninjured from risky military operations. I witnessed the most transcendent forms of solidarity, such as risking one's life for nothing in return, except for the pleasure of saving your comrade in danger. I also cried bitterly when on occasions I cared impotently for fighters who died in my arms in the prime of their youth, while I, with all my knowledge of health and disease was useless to prolong their life or even slow their dying.

I also saw the most despicable forms of human misery. One day, near Tecoluca in San Vicente, a village, guilty of some rebel stopping by occasionally in search of food, was invaded by the army. At night, several of the residents who had miraculously escaped the massacre came to our camp and asked us for help in finding and burying their dead. I saw children, dozens of children, disembowelled by bayonets, clinging, perhaps in their last gasp, to the corpses of their beheaded mothers. Picasso's Guernica and

[4] Margaret Whitehead, 'The concepts and principles of equity and health', *Health Promotion International*, vol. 6, no. 3, 1991, pp. 217–228.

Above. "In every fist raised by the people there is a smile, a rifle and the heart of Farabundo Martí. El Salvador needs you for victory. Join the revolutionary struggle. PC FAL"

Dante's Inferno pale before even the memory of those grisly scenes. These had been acts of terror against the population, carefully planned by colonels with immaculate uniforms at their gleaming desks. 'The guerrilla fighter moves among the population like a fish in water,' Colonel Domingo Monterrosa, Commander of the Atlacatl Battalion would say, 'and we have to take the water away from the fish so it drowns,' he would conclude.

Monterrosa was a diligent student of the U.S. military instructors who had trained him and his battalion of elite troops in counterinsurgency tactics learned in Vietnam. He was a seasoned military strategist who, unlike his comrades in arms, would accompany his troops on the ground. He was also as bloodthirsty as he was disciplined; he gained both experience and cruelty. He would design both a military operation and a torture session with the same precision.

After that day, there were many nights when I would awake upset, sweating and trembling. I had seen many wounded and dead during the war, as well as many victims of torture, but nothing like that. I would remember the mothers, but above all the children, all those children, each of them a life cut short, a promise unkept, a frustrated hope. Innocent voices suddenly silent, drowned in their own blood. Many nights I would remember the children; all those children were a recurring vision in which their corpses would come to life and they would reach out their arms to me demanding justice. So, I also hated. I learned to hate the culprit guilty of conceiving and executing that barbarity with mathematical precision.

Several years later, Domingo Monterrosa, the child killer, our Herod, at that time hero of the local oligarchy who had triumphed and won the admiration of his U.S. mentors, was killed by the rebels in Morazán. That day I threw a party in our camp. I was in Chalatenango, far from San Vicente, but in the village near our camp, the people sacrificed a cow and invited us to partake. We moved our entire party over there and danced until dawn. Then I strung up my hammock and slept peacefully for the first time in a long time. I never again had nightmares about the children of Tecoluca.

You think I have nothing of the romantic in me?

Judge for yourself by reading these poems, among the many I wrote that survived the war, the rain, the interminable marches, the persecution by the military, the helicopter transport landings and the aerial bombings.

Wellspring

As my eyes to the full moon
on this calm night in the mountains,
Thus I will divine your body among the shadows;

Like my revolutionary conscience
with the monthly tallying of enemy casualties,
Thus my heart will overflow with joy when you draw near;

With my finger on the trigger of my M-16[5]
when the time comes to break the enemy cordon,[6]
Thus my hands will caress your hair.

Like the barricades and Molotov cocktails
on the day of the insurrection,
Thus will your body burn in my arms.

Felipe D.[7],
August '86, Chalatenango

This one needs no explanation (I think).

Fear

With a calculated smile of contempt,
I stick close to the enemy and conspire under their noses;

With my conscience alone,
I defiantly confront (and defeat) the executioner and torture;

Certain of victory,
I enthusiastically await the next enemy operation;

5 The M-16 was the rifle that was part of my personal defence equipment. Even though we were medical personnel, we were no less pursued by the army.

6 The enemy cordon was the line of troops stretched out around a zone where the army suspected there were rebels. The cordon would tighten progressively in an attempt to hunt us down and the moment would come when we would have to fight to break through and escape the operation trying to annihilate our forces. The moments before were full of unspeakable tension.

7 Felipe Dubón was my nom de guerre. As a legacy from the urban underground struggle in the first years of the war, we did not use our own names, but rather pseudonyms.

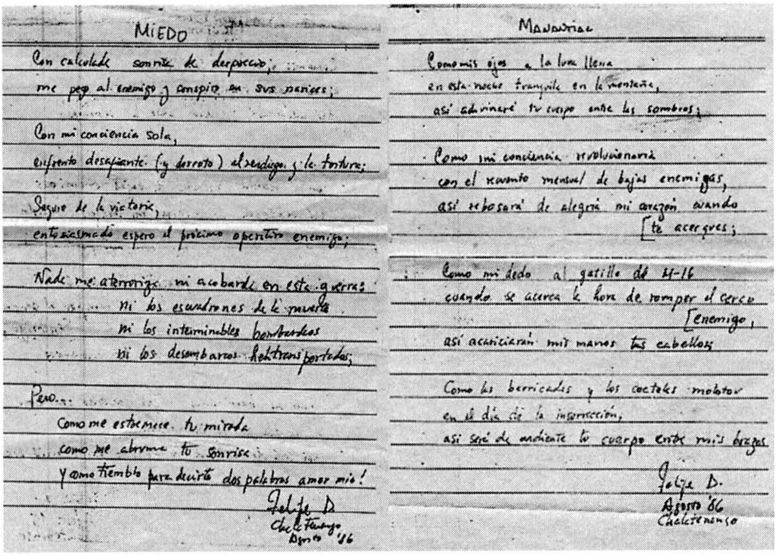

MIEDO

Con calculada sonrisa de desprecio,
me pego al enemigo y conspiro en sus narices;

Con mi conciencia sola,
enfrento desafiante (y derroto) al verdugo y la tortura;

Seguro de la victoria,
entusiasmado espero el próximo operativo enemigo;

Nada me aterroriza ni acobarda en esta guerra:
ni los escuadrones de la muerte
ni los interminables bombardeos
ni los desembarcos helitransportados;

Pero…
Como me estremece tu mirada
como me abruma tu sonrisa
y como tiemblo para decirte dos palabras amor mío!

Felipe D.
Chalatenango
Agosto '86

[illegible]

Como mis ojos a la luna llena
en esta noche tranquila en la montaña,
así adivinaré tu cuerpo entre las sombras;

Como mi conciencia revolucionaria
con el recuento mensual de bajas enemigas,
así rebosará de alegría mi corazón cuando
te acerques;

Como mi dedo al gatillo del M-16
cuando se acerca la hora de romper el cerco
enemigo,
así acariciarán mis manos tus cabellos;

Como las barricadas y los cocteles molotov
en el día de la insurrección,
así será de ardiente tu cuerpo entre mis brazos.

Felipe D.
Agosto '86
Chalatenango

Nothing terrifies or cows me in this war:
not the death squads
not the endless bombardments
not the helicopter landings

But . . .
How your gaze makes me shudder
How your smile overwhelms me
And how I tremble to tell you two words my love!

Felipe D.
August '86, Chalatenango

You say I have nothing of the romantic in me?

I rather think that I have too much. I've heard Luis Alberto say on more than one occasion that the Espinozas love without restraint or measure, that we give of ourselves completely and without duplicity. That has its pluses and its minuses. It marks us, not only us, but also whoever happens to be around us.

To what or to whom do we devote ourselves and make the target of our romanticism? Ah, that's a story for another day . . .

Affectionately,

Eduardo (or Felipe Dubón, the only way some remember me)

ELMER

I never knew how old he really was. Neither did he. He didn't even know the month and day he was born. When I realized that in his four years with the rebels he had never had a birthday I said: 'Elmer, from now on your birthday will be October 26th. We'll celebrate together since my birthday is also on that date. That way, neither one of us will forget. We'll tell everyone that you're twelve years old. What do you think?'

'Sure thing, *Compa* Felipe. And, how are we going to celebrate?'

'Well, let's see, the day before we'll go to a village, like Ojos de Agua, Vainillas, La Laguna or San Fernando, depending on where we are, and on our birthday we'll have a great big breakfast with fried eggs, salsa, beans, cream and toasted tortillas. With a little bit of luck, we'll even have pork cracklings.'

'And sweets?'

'Of course! All the sweets you can eat and all that you can stuff in your pockets.'

A satisfied smile spread over his childish face. He must have been around eleven or twelve then and for a year he'd been my courier and my guide over the countless paths and hills of Chalatenango. He never got lost. He would only have to walk a path once to be able to remember it perfectly months later, which I found admirable and at the same time incomprehensible. It was also very convenient, given my nonexistent sense of direction in the bush, which on several occasions made me the laughing stock of my *compañeros* at the front lines.

I saw him for the first time in 1985 when I entered the rebel-held territory in Chalatenango after I, together with 30 other political prisoners and close to 100 wounded combatants, was exchanged for the daughter of President José Napoleón Duarte. At that time, Elmer was travelling with a guerrilla logistics unit that had a couple of vehicles, which they used to transport weapons and supplies along the road from Zapotal to La Laguna, two villages in Chalatenango.

He was a bit pudgy, with a fair complexion, very light-brown hair and fine features. The veteran and hardened rebel fighters with whom he travelled treated him like a mascot, but absorbed as they were in the war and battles, they imposed strict military discipline on him. He would stand at attention before the unit leader, do a two to three hour morning workout, gather firewood, grind corn for tortillas, haul water and do all the jobs just like the other combatants, forfeiting the little time he had left as a child to developing his wits to compete for the few satisfactions of the Spartan guerrilla life, with seasoned combatants who tripled him in age, strength and experience. His life was constantly in danger, since the logistical troops he travelled with would frequently do battle against government army ambushes or patrols in the depths of guerrilla-held territory. The logistical troops also made dangerous contacts in Honduran territory to pick up weapons, provisions and other logistical supplies, which would occasionally lead to battles with special units of the Honduran army trained directly by U.S. advisers, who also coordinated, for these purposes, air and artillery support with their counterparts in the Salvadoran army.

One day of many when the transport unit was on its way to an assignment in Honduras, with Elmer along, I called over the unit leader.

'Ever,' I said, 'where did you get this kid from?'

'He was wandering around like a mule without a master, from camp to camp, and he got attached to us. The *compas* say he brings them good luck and the civilians really love him. Look, they make him uniforms, caps, a rucksack, everything. He's better equipped than we are!'

Above. 24 October 1985, Tenancingo. Exchange of prisoners for the daughter of President Duarte.

'Sure, but any time now they're going to kill him in battle. Wouldn't it be better to leave him in a hamlet with the people?'

'We already tried that, *Compa* Felipe, but he always comes back to one of the camps and then he looks for us. The civilians we've left him with say that when he sees soldiers he goes white, pure white, and can't stop shaking.'

'Okay, let's do something then. Send him over to Health and I'll talk to Rosalí and have her set him up with the hospital couriers. At least he'll be safer there.'

The Frente Couriers

The hospital had three or four couriers, known as *correos*, usually too young to fight, who would deliver messages back and forth among the different health posts and the zone command. These were the '*Correos del Frente*' (sort of a rebel postal service) who together with their peers from the other commands and units formed a very special and appreciated platoon. Not only would they travel quickly and alone; their job demanded a thorough knowledge of the terrain and they also had to be disciplined and absolutely trustworthy.

Above. 24 October 1985, Tenancingo. Exchange of prisoners for the daughter of President Duarte.

Their equipment was a handheld torch, a rain poncho and a plastic envelope or bag to keep the sensitive and strategic messages they were delivering dry and undamaged. Depending on the need, they would go out at any time of day or night and were gifted with a particular and sharp sense of direction, even on the darkest nights. On many nights, while we made coffee around a discrete fire in the mountains, I enjoyed listening to their youthful conversations, telling anecdotes about the vicissitudes of their jobs or competing with each other over whose torch was the best, measured by the ability to concentrate light and shine it the farthest.

It only took two weeks for Rosalí, the head of the hospital, to come to my tent to complain bitterly about Elmer.

'*Compa*, I can't take him anymore! I've come to ask you to transfer him. He fights with all the couriers. He won't obey me or anyone else. He doesn't want to attend any of the classes and he tells me he won't take orders from women.'

'Okay, then send him to me. Tell him he's going to be my courier.'

The next day he arrived at six in the morning, impeccably

clean and uniformed, and he saluted me challengingly, asking for instructions on his new assignment.

'*Compañero* Felipe, I am reporting that they have transferred me here with instructions to put myself at your orders.'

From the outset, I enjoyed listening to how serious and disciplined he was at such a young age. It would be a long time before I would associate that first impression of his attitude with his lacerating and shocking past.

'At ease, *compañero* Elmer,' I said with the same seriousness. 'Starting today you will be my guide and my courier. Tomorrow we leave for San Fernando and then to Arcatao.'

Some time had already passed since 'Salvador Guerra'[1] had sent for me to give me my new duties after letting me rest for a few days on the banks of the Sumpul River.

Time went by very slowly in the pools of the Sumpul River and I had begun to feel somewhat ashamed at not really having anything to do two months after getting out of the Mariona prison, especially because I had recently heard about the death on the Guazapa volcano of César, an ex-priest who was a member of the ERP.[2] We'd become very good friends in Mariona and had gotten out of prison together as part of the exchange for Duarte's daughter. I learned he'd been captured wounded in an invasion and had been decapitated.

'We have a long border with Honduras,' Salvador explained to me, 'and we're not making the best use of it. We need to develop logistical routes and supply lines for the troops, in addition to safe routes to evacuate or bring in strategic personnel or for members of the High Command to leave the country when they need to. This will be your new job. We already sent for Auri, who is in charge of the work in Honduras, to nail down your work with you.

1 Atilio Montalvo, an astute guerrilla commander who designed 'low-altitude anti-aircraft warfare' to successfully fight the helicopters.

2 Ejército Revolucionario del Pueblo (People's Revolutionary Army), one of the five guerrilla organizations making up the FMLN.

She should be showing up soon.'

A couple of days later, Auri arrived at our camp. I had known her briefly during my days as an urban guerrilla in the late 1970s, but had lost track of her since then. Auri was a surrealistic vision in the midst of those rugged mountains where the only thing that was plentiful was scarcity. When I saw her come out of her tent I refused to believe what I was seeing. She looked like she had just stepped out of a hotel lobby or some bank bureaucrat's office. Her skin and her hands were smooth and fine, her nails were neat, carefully manicured and polished. Her long hair was pulled back and perfectly coiffed and I couldn't see a single wrinkle on her immaculate dress, which looked like it had just been picked up from the drycleaner's.

'Hi Felipe,' she said when she saw me, 'what time shall we get to work?'

'After breakfast,' I answered. 'We have a lot to talk about.'

After eating our usual morning ration of boiled beans with two corn tortillas we sat down in front of a set of 1:5,000 scale maps of the border, an incredibly valuable gift Auri had brought me. At the front, this could only be obtained after a battle in which the enemy leadership had been wiped out or captured and their military equipment requisitioned, which invariably contained map sets of this type, representing both a valuable war trophy and a strategic tool for planning troop movements over the terrain.

We spent two days and most of the nights by dim candlelight going over in detail access routes from Honduras, Honduran border highways and local roads, hamlets and settlements, Honduran collaborators and their customs, dangerous spots, Honduran army checkpoints, their usual routes for mobilization, and our vehicles with their '*embutidos*'.[3] She then gave me a thorough description of

[3] Ingenious double-bottomed compartments, installed in different locations depending on the type of vehicle, masterpieces of Salvadoran and Honduran handiwork that successfully evaded the meticulous searches by Honduran troops to detect them, soldiers that were directly trained by U.S. troops

the guerrilla history of each of our select drivers of these strategic vehicles, including their love affairs and personal weaknesses, as well as the '*tatús*' assigned to each one to store the materials they were transporting when delivery was not made directly to our logistics troops.

The logistics platoon had very particular characteristics. Everyone had to be battle hardened and be very solid ideologically. Their job was very sensitive and if they were taken prisoner, which occasionally happened, they had to have the ability to resist being tortured, to not betray their Honduran collaborators or the logistics routes, or reveal the content and location of their *tatús* or the *embutidos* in their vehicles.

They were almost always ex-combatants from the Special Select Forces or the Vanguard Unit[4] who had been wounded and couldn't continue fighting. The drivers of the vehicles or those who were in charge of safe houses along the logistics route in Honduras were almost always from an urban background, while those who would pick up and transport the materials that were brought across the border, such as the guerrillas who had 'adopted' Elmer, were almost always from the rural countryside.

The day that Auri was to leave for Honduras, I returned from bathing in the river at six in the morning and was intrigued to see Elmer chatting with two other couriers with whom he habitually fought. They all had their slingshots with them, which they usually used to hunt wild birds to add some protein to our monotonous diet of tortillas and beans. When they saw me they looked surprised

stationed at the U.S. Palmerola Air Base in Honduras to fight the Sandinistas and the Salvadoran revolutionaries.

[4] The Vanguard Units were made up of the bravest and most skilful combatants, who were also the most dedicated and had leadership qualities, which made them stand out from the other troops. The Special Select Forces were carefully chosen from among the best combatants and commanders of the Vanguard Units. They were the crème de la crème of the guerrilla forces and it was a privilege and a spectacle to see one of their training sessions and to observe them operating in combat against the enemy. Each one was a weapon with a precision and lethality that were simply impressive.

and alarmed, which made me suspicious.

After I took down my tarp tent I decided to take another look and just as I turned around, they were taking aim with their slingshots at a wasp nest that was right over Auri's tent. Naturally, the highly effective aim of Elmer and his followers bore immediate fruit, and left me no time to order them to stop. With the first concentrated volley, the nest came down, and almost immediately poor Auri emerged terrified and ran around the entire camp half naked, pursued by the wasps and by the laughter of Elmer and his cronies.

The joke was also costly for Elmer: seizure of his slingshot, three hours of lookout duty for 15 nights and 50 additional jumping jacks after finishing his morning callisthenics, although perhaps what cost and hurt him the most was having to apologize to Auri as a condition for suspending the jumping jacks penalty. Elmer resisted this to the last moment, but he finally gave in when, en route to Honduras, we accompanied Auri to the border town of San Fernando a few days later.

Auri, whose deceptive appearance did not reveal her solidarity, deep sensitivity and other unexpected characteristics when judged only by her looks, developed a special affection for Elmer from that time on. Whenever she returned to the northern front she would bestow small gifts and treats upon him that would delight Elmer, and he in turn would blush from genuine shame any time he was reminded of the wasp-nest episode.

The Thousand and One Nights

I would spend the next several months with Elmer and Dimas (the *compañero* who was assigned to my security) walking over and over again from San Fernando in north-western Chalatenango to Arcatao in the department's northeast corner. We would usually camp alone, far from the guerrilla encampments and very close to the Honduran border, since a good part of our work consisted of 'attending'[5] Honduran collaborators.

On one of the rare occasions that we spent the night in an insurgent camp, near Nueva Trinidad, it caught my eye when one of the rebels took out a thick old book from his rucksack and carefully ripped out two pages. It was rare to find a book in those remote places so I asked him to lend it to me to leaf through it. It turned out to be a version of *The Thousand and One Nights* that the guerrilla fighter was using as loo paper and by this time some fifty pages were already missing.

'Listen, Javier,' I said to him after I realized the unfortunate destination the Persian classic would continue to have in his hands, 'won't you trade that book of yours for a loo roll that I have here? It's much softer and besides, you'd be doing me a favour because I want to read the book.'

'Sure thing, *Compa* Felipe,' he said eagerly when he saw my interest, 'I'll swap it for the loo roll and ten cigarettes.'

'It's a deal!' I said. 'Here's the roll and the cigarettes.'

A couple of days later we began a routine that would break up the usual monotony of our tedious hikes along the Honduran border. I became a modern Scheherazade and assumed the task of telling Elmer the adventures of the legendary characters during our walks, after having refreshed the forgotten stories I vaguely remembered from my childhood, reading by night the book whose wretched future had been redeemed by a roll of loo paper and ten cigarettes. The deal with Javier cost my petit bourgeois backside a week of discomfort before I could get to a town and buy a new roll, but it was worth it.

Nightfall and not the dawn would interrupt my tales and it was Elmer who would unfailingly demand I continue each morning when we set off on the trail.

[5] In guerrilla slang, this meant giving them ideological support, keeping them informed about the course of the war in El Salvador, orienting them on how to recruit new collaborators, supervising completion of their assignments and channelling their contributions to the Salvadoran revolutionaries.

'*Compa* Felipe, we left off when Ali Baba was opening the cave of the thieves.' Or, 'Yesterday we stopped when Sinbad the Sailor was starting his second voyage.'

Well-seasoned Dimas enjoyed the tales as much or more than Elmer, watching us and listening, as well as making well-timed comments that set Elmer's imagination alight.

'Isn't it true *Compa* Felipe that that Ali Baba was towheaded just like Elmer?'

During our free time, I had fruitlessly tried to teach him to read, appealing to his deep-seated military discipline.

'Elmer,' I said one day, 'the commanders' couriers need to know how to read, so we're going to start tomorrow. I've gotten a notebook and a ballpoint pen. You'll have two hours of class every day.'

However, there was no way to motivate him. Elmer had already had one failed attempt, the result of a request to my son Jaime to teach him to read. But it mortified him that Jaime, with whom he was vying for my affection, would be the one to do so. Nevertheless, it was precisely the stories from the Orient and his imagination, spurred on by Dimas's witty commentaries, that were the magic formula for him to learn to read, something I was able to achieve in the mutilated book that I ended up giving him. Learning to read was an unsuspecting adventure for him; it made me earn his respect and his love. Years later when we were in Metapán, when responding to his request to look for some maps in his rucksack, I would be proud and pleasantly surprised to find the book, well kept and carefully wrapped in a plastic bag to protect it from the elements. The long hikes and the fight for survival in the war had taught us to value every gram that we put in our rucksacks and everything we carried was just what was necessary, such that a book like that one, heavy and certainly no longer read, gave witness to his affection and his emotional ties to our treks years earlier.

Suchitlán

One day, when I went to the command post to report on my work on the border, we stopped at a guerrilla camp in the mountains around the village of Dulce Nombre de María. I was intrigued to see how Elmer gave up his usual one-man tent to bunk with another rebel.

It wasn't until the next day that I was surprised to see the huge resemblance between them. Elmer saw my surprise and explained.

'*Compa* Felipe, I'm going to introduce you to my brother.'

He was perhaps 17 or 18 years old, thin, average height with an intelligent and alert gaze. He greeted me cordially and unabashedly and several hours later we ran into each other in the camp's kitchen while waiting for our tortillas.

'Hi,' I said. 'I was talking to Héctor (at the time, the leader of his battalion) and he said that you're already a squadron leader because you're a good guerrilla fighter.'

'I guess I'm just a bit lucky in combat,' he said, smiling with pride.

Then he tensed up a bit and said: '*Compa*, I want to thank you for educating Elmer. He told me he can read fluently. He says you taught him. And he also writes better than I do. I think he's completely cured.'

'Cured? What is he cured from? He never seemed sick to me.'

'Of the muteness, *Compa*. He went mute when they killed our family. He spent two years without saying a word.'

'Tell me, what happened? Where?'

'Well, you see, we were living in Copapayo on the banks of the Suchitlán reservoir. I was about as old as Elmer is now and Elmer was really little. My father was out working in the cornfield and had sent me fishing. I took Elmer with me so he could learn. By prayer time[6] we were already on our way home. It was getting dark, which is why the soldiers didn't see us.'

'The soldiers?'

'Yes. When we got there they were inside the house and in the yard in front. Elmer and I hid on the shore among the water hyacinths on the lake. From there we could see that they had tied up my father and they were beating him. They were yelling at him that he was a guerrilla and they gave it to him, the poor soul, with their rifle butts. My mother tried to defend him and that's when they killed her in a burst of rifle fire. They killed her first. Elmer was in front of me and when he saw that they'd killed our mother he cried out. Luckily he wasn't very loud because if he had been, they would have killed us, too. That's when I grabbed him around his chest with one arm so he couldn't move and with the other hand I covered his mouth, because a soldier had become suspicious and was on alert and turned to look in our direction, but we were lucky and he didn't see us. Elmer was trembling. His whole body was shaking and I was squeezing harder and harder on his mouth so that he wouldn't scream. I didn't realize that I was squeezing him so hard because they were killing the entire family. First they cut off my father's head in front of my brothers and sisters and then they killed my sister, the one after me who was a little older than Elmer. Then my two little brothers who were younger than Elmer. They stabbed them to death. People say that they must have gone straight to heaven because they were so little and hadn't sinned yet.'

[6] An old custom that refers to the family gathering in the field at the end of the workday to give thanks to God. It persists as a synonym for sunset or nightfall.

'And how did you two save yourselves?'

'Miraculously, *Compa*. Since the soldiers didn't leave, we scurried out into the lake and grabbed on to a pretty big tree branch. That's when I realized that my hand was bleeding. I'd squeezed Elmer so tight that his teeth had dug into my hand and I hadn't even realized it. Look, you can still see the scar. The wound got infected. I was in the hospital for almost two months getting treatment because it kept oozing pus. I think it was from it being wet for so long, because we swam all night long, hanging on to the branch, until we got to the other side of the lake. Poor Elmer wasn't shaking from fright anymore, but from the cold.'

'And when did Elmer start talking again?'

'Like I said, it took two years. He'd just use gestures to make himself understood. It was after a bombardment in San Antonio Los Ranchos that he spoke. Like they say, "one nail drives out another nail" and the fright from the bombardment drove the other fright out of Elmer. The bombs were falling on us like it was raining. Those demons practically killed us. They wanted to finish off the entire family.'

'And when did you join the guerrillas?'

'A little after Elmer started talking again. He was older and didn't really need to be taken care of. Plus, I was also more grown up and I wanted to get even for what happened to my family, although *compa* Héctor tells us that we are not in this for revenge and that the soldiers are like us only that the rich folks have confused them. But I say that if they were only mixed up, they wouldn't kill children or women. We didn't kill their families, only them, and that was only in combat. When they surrender, we respect their lives. We only take their uniforms and their boots in addition to their weapons, but we don't kill them. We don't even beat them. We turn them over to the Red Cross. What do you say *Compa*? They're evil, aren't they?'

A call from his superior to get into formation saved me from a long and perhaps not very convincing answer to his questions.

Shortly after lunch, Elmer, Dimas and I began the hike to the border. We'd been walking about half an hour when Elmer's brother caught up to us sweating and panting.

'*Compa* Felipe,' he said, 'I have something for you.'

He unbuckled his military belt and slipped off a canteen nested inside a stainless steel cup, both wrapped in a cover made out of very strong synthetic fabric. This military gear was highly coveted and valuable among the insurgent ranks, supplied to the government army by U.S. military aid. The canteen was indispensable and you could cook anything in the versatile cup, from coffee to soup. Whoever had them had necessarily commandeered them from an enemy who had died in combat or from the prisoners. They were a trophy of war.

'Why don't you give it to Elmer instead,' I said. 'I'm sure he'll use it more than I will.'

'No, *Compa*, it's for you. It's a memento. It's so you can impress the girls. Elmer isn't on the make yet. When he becomes a guerrilla fighter, let him take one.'

Then he turned to Elmer.

'And you, behave yourself and listen to *compa* Felipe. Learn things that will be useful to you so you can be a good guerrilla fighter and so you're not thinking about mischief.'

Then he went back the way he had come as fast as he had appeared and I never saw him again.

Elmer and Weapons

When Elmer joined the *Correos del Frente* as a courier he brought with him a valuable gift he'd been given by his previous unit, the logistics platoon – a sawed-off M-16 rifle. It looked like a toy but it was an authentic rifle that had half of its barrel cut off in a rebel workshop. Since the rifle was so snub-nosed, many people made fun of it, but Elmer was always ready to explain and would say: 'Did you know that this rifle has a harder kick than a big one and is louder than a big one?'

And in effect it was. I had not heard it until one night when Elmer was on sentry duty in the middle of the night and a thunderous burst of fire from his rifle woke us all up. We grabbed our weapons and, alarmed, began to search around the camp, since Elmer said he'd shot at three men who were sneaking up and who didn't obey his order to halt. Two hours later, tired and falling asleep we opted for reinforcing the lookouts and resting a little while longer until the sun came up. After daybreak, the best trackers in our camp thoroughly inspected the surroundings.

'There are no human footprints. And no cattle have come through here either. That kid on lookout duty is just making things up,' was the report from the exploration squad.

Confronted by our questions and contradicting himself, Elmer had no other choice than to admit that he had fired without justification. It turned out that he had only fired his weapon on two occasions during a training course and he wanted to know 'if the rifle was still good'.

The prank cost him the weapon. As punishment for this serious breach he was relieved of his weapon and sent to the kitchens to grind corn and haul water for a week, with no chance of getting the rifle back 'until he demonstrated responsibility' and 'earned the weapon back again'.

In late 1986, I was transferred to Metapán, in north-western El Salvador. The zone was very dangerous because there were no rebel strongholds there. The region was teeming with civil defence officers and there were many fixed army posts. The death squads operated with impunity and intensely and the local population was very afraid as a result of the massacres perpetrated by the army in the area following the rebel offensive of 1981, in which they had killed several hundred people indiscriminately.

On this occasion, it was 'Chele Dimas' (Commander Dimas Rodríguez, second in charge and military strategist for the FPL) who explained my assignment.

'Look Felipe, we need a little more stability in the strategic rear guard to be able to prepare more destructive blows to the enemy. Among other things, we need to tie up the Second Brigade – based in Santa Ana – because now, every time the army invades Chalatenango or San Vicente, they bring them along as reinforcements. The only way to do this is by increasing our operations there; but to do so, we need to rebuild the mass movement so that it can nourish our forces.

'Okay, but I understand that "Carabina"[7] is there. What's up with him?'

'The problem is that the west is too big and Orlando is more involved in building up forces in Ahuachapán, Sonsonate and the city of Santa Ana. We need someone to take charge of the northern part of the department to develop a strategic rear guard for that front and we have thought of you for that job. See,' he explained over a map of the zone, 'Texistepeque, Masahuat, Santa Rosa Guachipilín and especially Metapán will become increasingly important as the war expands. Metapán not only borders on Chalatenango, it shares characteristics with the north: pine forests, mountains and a lot of support from the local people. Right now they're somewhat quiet because of the massacres that happened and because we haven't had a presence there, but if we're smart, we can rebuild what we had and militarily and politically upset the enemy.'

[7] Orlando 'Carabina', a charismatic long-time fighter and grassroots organizer.

'Alright, I'll see what I can do,' I told him. 'And what forces do I have for this work?'

'There are two party members,' he answered. 'Alonso, from the city and experienced in mass organizing, and Andrés Guerrero, a local fellow who knows the zone like the palm of his hand and is very experienced in combat. There is also a small guerrilla column.'

'That's it?' I said, a bit taken aback. 'I thought we'd be a little better off.'

'Well, that's the task – to get us in better shape to tie up the Second Brigade.'

Elmer did not hesitate to come with me when I told him he was free to stay in Chalate or to go with me. Dimas (my security guard) excused himself from going because his family was in Chalate and his wife had just given birth, but he offered to escort me to the location of the Western Front command post.

Three days after leaving the Montañona where I had met with Dimas, we got to Cerro La Gloria in the extreme southwest of Chalatenango, to Orlando's camp.

Orlando was cheerful, folksy, beloved by the rebel fighters and he also played the guitar very well. He was surprised that I'd gotten there so quickly and told me that the guerrilla column from Metapán was present right then in a political-military course. I sent Elmer to inspect the column while I worked with Orlando on the situation in Metapán.

'There are only five of them and they're all rookies, *Compa* Felipe,' Elmer told me when he returned. 'They don't know how to clean or disassemble the rifles and they are learning to shoot because they don't know how to do that either.'

'Did you see Andrés?'

'Yes, he seems really sharp. He's the leader and he's the one teaching the others.'

Two days later we met up with them as they were walking towards Metapán, with Andrés and Alonso at the head of our brand new guerrilla column, made up of our five enthusiastic novice fighters.

When we arrived at a settlement called Las Almohadas, in the municipality of Masahuat, where several rebel sympathisers lived and which would be our base of operations, we realized just how difficult the situation was. We hid and slept during the day and at night we'd walk down to visit the other settlements to try to rebuild the organization that the army and the death squads had mercilessly decimated. There were many *orejas* (informers) and it didn't take the army long to find out that we were hanging around there. The situation got more complicated and dangerous and we would frequently engage in combat, which is why I decided to give Elmer a pistol to give him a modicum of security.

A couple of months later we were in a vast pasture and we decided to get water from a watering hole. We would often have to compete with the cattle for water, since these manmade ponds were the only option. As the dry season wore on and other sources dried up, the rivalry grew more intense. The army knew that sooner or later we'd go to the cattle ponds and had them under surveillance.

We were filling our canteens when Andrés sounded the alarm.

'The army's coming, with about 60 troops (there were just six of us) and they are manoeuvring to surround us from the south,' he said. 'We have to get to the ravine before they cut off the retreat in that direction. If we get there, we'll be safe.'

'Let's go,' I said. 'We'll retreat in staggered groups. Andrés, Alonso and the radio operator will form one group and Ever (another Ever, not Elmer's old superior), Elmer and I will make up the other group.'

The radio operator and Elmer had handguns and the other four of us had M-16 rifles. Almost as soon as we began to leave the watering hole, the first soldiers started firing at us. We answered their fire according to our plan to move in staggered groups. While one group fired to hold off the army's advance, the other ran to the next position on the path to the ravine. In less than 20 minutes and under heavy rifle fire we managed to get to the rim of the ravine. Andrés's group was the first to arrive and begin to walk down into the gully where the vegetation was thick. Then Elmer and I began the walk downhill while Ever took refuge behind a tree and continued firing.

'Hurry up Ever,' I said, 'we're all safe now.'

'You go on, *Compa*, I'll be right behind you. I just want to take care of that little scumbag with the grenade launcher.'

We continued to race downhill toward the thicket, but when we got to the bottom of the ravine, Ever was not behind us.

'I'll go see if something happened to him,' Elmer told me and took off running back uphill.

'Elmer! Get back here, they're going to kill you!' I said, to no avail.

The fire power of his pistol was a joke compared not only to the number of army troops, who outnumbered us ten to one, but also to their high-powered rifles and grenade launchers. He didn't have a chance against them. The fire fight raged. They'd surely located Elmer and were concentrating their fire in his direction. I tried to go look for him, but when I got up to the rim of the ravine, a hail of gunfire erupted around me, forcing me to retreat. Shortly after, I joined Andrés's group. Distraught, I thought that Ever and Elmer were certainly already dead or wounded in their lopsided combat against the army.

As expected, the army didn't dare to follow us into the ravine for fear that we would ambush them, so we decided to stop to rest a bit and plan our movements better. We were at work when we heard someone approaching. We spread out and hid behind some rocks preparing for a new battle, when we saw not the army, but Elmer appear, acting as Ever's guide dog.

Ever's face was completely covered in blood and he couldn't see a thing. Then he told us that when he was hiding behind the tree an enemy bullet hit the chamber of his rifle and wounded his face. When I examined his right eye, I saw that it had been destroyed by a shard from the rifle. His other eye was fine, but the bleeding from his right eye had blinded him and up until then he thought he was totally blind.

Later he told us how Elmer had rescued him in the midst of the gunfire and threw him into the ravine while he continued to fire at the army with his pistol. He then caught up with Ever and guided him until they found us.

The next day I publicly congratulated Elmer in front of the rest of our unit for his heroism. He was beside himself with pride and only had one comment to make.

'*Compa* Felipe?'

'Yes.'

'Isn't it true that I've earned my rifle back?'

Two days later he was given an M-16 rifle, which from then on he carried with exemplary responsibility.

Leave-taking

By 1988, and as a result of all our organizing work in Metapán, the development of the revolutionary forces in the zone was more than evident. The initial collective conformed by Andrés Guerrero, Alonso, Elmer and myself had reproduced to levels unthinkable in relation to the expectations and mood of scepticism when we arrived. By this time, we had two guerrilla columns of some 30 combatants each, a vanguard unit of 15 combatants and around 500 militia members, in addition to the whole organizational structure that involved thousands of people in different movements.

We had shut down the civil defence and we could move around the entire zone with relative security. Our force's operations were so intense and far-reaching that the Second Brigade could no longer travel to reinforce operations against our troops in Chalatenango or San Vicente, as they had frequently done before. They were forced to deconcentrate their three battalions and had to stick to local terrain. One battalion was posted to the cement works, one to the Guajoyo dam and the third to the department's capital city.

Every three weeks, there was a rotation of the enemy positions and the battalion from the cement works would come down parallel to the road, scouring the terrain. Our forces would take advantage of this situation to harass and ambush them, causing them casualties. This relocation of government forces required constant movement of army convoys on the highway from Santa Ana to Metapán. The convoys were particularly coveted targets of guerrilla attacks, because the army was concentrated and vulnerable, and even when the vehicles were armoured, we could always use more explosives in the mines, enough to destroy them or stop their advance and wage battle against them. Every week, we'd mount at least one ambush and government casualties were increasingly significant.

All this produced a sigh of relief in our strategic rear guard in Chalatenango and San Vicente. Chele Dimas even visited the zone to personally convey the congratulations of the General Command for the successful accomplishment of our mission. In a second stage, we made an incursion into and consolidated the mountainous region of Metapán, we opened the corridor to Chalatenango and we increased our operations to such a level that the government army even targeted us with elite battalion raids. The work had now taken on its own momentum and growth, leading me to foresee that the leadership would soon change my job, which happened in late 1988, when I was persuaded to leave Metapán to assume a new mission outside the country.

By then, it had been a year since Elmer had stopped being my courier and guide. He had very respectfully but also very firmly expressed his desire to join the fighting forces and asked for a transfer. Once he joined one of our guerrilla columns, he quickly stood out for his bravery, level-headedness and knowledge of the enemy, as well as for his initiative on the battlefield. He was promoted to squadron leader and in the space of six months he had already joined the vanguard unit. Whenever he had some free

Above. Drawing by a child who survived the Copapayo massacre, perpetrated by the Atlacatl Battalion.

time, he would visit me in my camp and we would talk at length about different topics such as the course of the war, his aspirations and his future.

When I was notified of my transfer, I sent for him.

'Elmer,' I began, 'I'll be leaving the country and I have requested and have obtained authorization to take you with me. I think this is a good time for you to study more, and that way you could serve the revolution better. What do you say? Would you like to go with me? We'll be reunited with Jaime. (A couple of years older than Elmer, my son Jaime had left the front and was going to school, but he had also joined a guerrilla collective outside the country, working in his free time repairing guerrilla communication radios and other electronic devices.) The city is also a war front and there is a lot to be done there.'

'Look, *Compa*, I really would like to go to school and contribute more, but the thing is that I have a girlfriend and we're about to move in together.'

'Ah! And who is your girlfriend, if I may ask?'

'The unit's radio operator.[8] You know her.'

'Of course I know her! She's delightful! No wonder you're so in love. Well, think it over well and talk to her about it, and then let me know what you two decide.'

Elmer's face was a rainbow while he told me about his love affair with the radio operator and how excited they both were. A couple of days later he came to see me and tell me his decision. He had decided to stay and move in with his sweetheart.

'*Compa*, don't forget about me and write to me now and then. We have to see each other again. I want to tell you something. The thing is, no matter how much I try, I haven't been able to remember what my father was like, but I'm sure he must have been like you.'

Elmer and two other fighters from his squadron escorted me on the long hike to Guatemala, where I exited through a logistics corridor that we'd opened a little to the south of Lake Guajoyo. After making contact with our collaborator in Guatemala, Hilario Calderón, an elderly guerrilla who had settled in Jutiapa where he could provide us with support along the logistics route, the time finally came for us to say goodbye.

Our eyes misted up as we embraced tightly. As I watched him walk off, I noticed his gallant bearing, reflected among other details in his impeccable military uniform that looked tailor made. He also wore an olive green cap and a military harness, holsters for his rifle's magazines, his canteen, cup and military boots. All this had been commandeered in different battles and it was high-quality gear, the kind used by army officers in the Second Brigade. I imagined the proud smile that would have been on his brother's face while watching him if he'd been there and I smiled in turn. That's the last image I have of him since I never saw him again.

In November 1989, the Salvadoran guerrillas began their strategic offensive to pressure the process toward the peace

[8] Responsible for operational communications, the right hand of the military leader in battle, radio operators encrypted and decrypted coded messages at incredible speed.

accords. By then, I was in Nicaragua and aware of the numerous war dispatches that were coming into the nerve centre that was the focal point of all the communications taking place with the commanders of our forces, which were fighting across El Salvador.

As much as I tried, I had not been able to make it back to El Salvador in time to participate in the offensive. When I got to Managua and was just about to return to El Salvador the commanders stopped me, because some information about the preparations for the offensive had leaked out to the government, which had reinforced security at airports and border crossings. This put me in a position of extreme vulnerability since I was included on all the government's watch lists because of the two times I'd been captured and the fact that when I was exchanged for the president's daughter, my name was second on the list demanded by the rebels, right after Hugo, a fellow prisoner in Mariona Prison, who was the second in command in the Communist Party, after Schafik Handal.

When I was informed of the decision to not send me to El Salvador, based on the risks to myself and to the organization if I went, I specifically asked to join the communications hub to strengthen it during the offensive, where we were involved in feverish activity day and night. Thus, I would receive first hand, consolidated daily, our victories and our defeats, our positions and those of the government army, the casualties caused to the enemy as well as our own. Of course I paid particular attention to the news from Metapán.

Several days after the offensive began, when I heard his name among the casualties in northern Santa Ana, I wanted to believe that it was another Elmer. But the next day, a special message came in from the western front asking 'to notify Felipe Dubón that his courier from Chalatenango had fallen while fighting in Metapán'.

Elmer fell in combat near the city. At the head of his squadron, he had organized an ambush of an enemy patrol on the road out of Metapán to Santa Ana and in the ensuing clash with army reinforcements, one of his combatants was wounded. He could have saved himself, but as the exemplary military leader that he was, he attempted to rescue the wounded man, and was hit by government fire when he did.

Even today, I don't know exactly what his name was, or how old he was when he died, but every 26th of October, on our birthday, I remember him very fondly.

GLOSSARY

campesino/a: Rural peasant farmer or farm-worker.
compa: Shortened form of *compañero/a.*
compañero/a: Comrade, from the Spanish word for companion.
Chalate: Shortened form of Chalatenango.
department: Administrative division. El Salvador is divided into 14 departments.
Farabundo Martí: A revolutionary leader in El Salvador during the 1932 peasant uprising. The FMLN adopted his name.
FMLN: Frente Farabundo Martí para la Liberación Nacional (Farabundo Martí National Liberation Front): the coalition of five insurgent groups that waged war against the repressive Salvadoran regime throughout the 1980s (FPL, RN, PRTC, ERP, PC).
guerrillero: Rebel fighter.
guinda: Tactical retreats on foot to flee the advance of the military.
hacienda: A large estate or plantation with a dwelling house.
Hospital del Frente: FMLN military hospital. The highest level of care in the war zone.
masas: Politically committed civilians, from the Spanish word for masses.
sanitario/a: Medics.
tatú: Concealed underground chambers of varying architecture and capacity depending on their use (to house and protect provisions, medicines, weapons, supplies, wounded combatants), with a very well-camouflaged entrance that completely blended in with the surroundings to keep them from being located during government incursions into rebel-held territory. Their design and materials and the mechanisms for opening and closing them could be highly sophisticated in urban locations or more rustic in the rural guerrilla forces.

APPENDIX:
LETTER FROM A SON

To: Eduardo Espinoza <eduardo@xxx.xxx>
From: Jaime Espinoza <jajaen@xxx.xxx>
8 October 2007 15:43
Subject: From the Shadows to the Light

Papá,

I want to thank you for sending me the news about your book, and congratulate you for the great effort you've made.

I want to tell you that among the hundreds of pages that I have to read, I'm making the time to read the stories you've sent me, and I don't want to stop until I've finished them all.

You've made me remember many things. It's incredible how we lived, with so little. That lump in my throat, accompanied by tears, won't go away.

I remember when we were leaving the Felde family mansion in Nicaragua, where the communications HQ was, and you gave me the news that Elmer had fallen in combat. That made me sad. Now that I remember it again, I feel even sadder, because Elmer, like me, believed that all that was normal, that there was no other way to live other than with a tarp to sleep on and our food in our hands.

Thank you for remembering my brothers: Andrés and Elmer. I didn't manage to spend much time with either of them, but even so, their departure hurts. Neither should have died.

Grandma Mina, who will probably cry just as I have when she reads these pages, must feel fortunate. She was lucky enough to cry from happiness when she saw you return many years later, unlike thousands and thousands of mothers who only saw their sons depart.

Thank you for moving the fallen from the shadows to the light.

Hugs,

Jaime